DEVIL'S NIGHT

DEVIL'S NIGHT

CURTIS M. LAWSON

Trade Paperback Edition

All stories are original to this collection.

Text © 2021 by Curtis M. Lawson

Cover and interior art © 2021 by Luke Spooner

ISBN: 978-1-888993-16-5

Editor & Publisher, Joe Morey

Copy editing and interior design by F. J. Bergmann

Weird House Press
Central Point, OR 97502
www.weirdhousepress.com

I extend my deepest gratitude to the following for their help in shaping this book ... Joe Morey and the team at Weird House Press, S. T. Joshi, Luke Spooner, G. D. Dearborn, Gregor Xane, Joshua Rex, Duncan Ralston, John Chesnut, Michael Cushing, George Illet Anderson, Robb Kavjian, and Mark Matthews.

An extra special thanks to Christine and Tristan for their constant love, patience, and support.

List of Illustrations

Devil's Night (detail)	viii
Trash-Fire Stories	xiv
D20	16
Devil's Tongue	36
No One Leaves the Butcher Shop	54
Fire Sermon	72
A Night of Art and Excess	100
Rashaam the Unholy	130
An Angel in Amber Leaves	160
The Exorcism of Detroit, Michigan	178

Table of Contents

Introduction — ix

Trash-Fire Stories — 1

D20 — 17

Devil's Tongue — 37

No One Leaves the Butcher Shop — 55

Fire Sermon — 73

Through Hell for One Kiss — 77

Breaking Wheel — 85

A Night of Art and Excess — 101

The Work of the Devil — 119

Rashaam the Unholy — 131

The Graveyard of Charles Robert Swede — 133

This City Needs Jesus — 145

An Angel in Amber Leaves — 161

The Exorcism of Detroit, Michigan — 179

About the Author — 197

About the Artist — 199

Introduction

My first introduction to Devil's Night, like that of many people, came from *The Crow*. The dark visuals of the grim cityscape juxtaposed with the blazing gold and amber flames burned themselves into my imagination. It wasn't just the imagery that enthralled me, of course. There was also the concept—a night without law or hope, a night where the real-life bad guys came out like monsters beneath a smoke-choked black sky, unafraid and unashamed. It terrified me. That was, to me, a much scarier concept than Halloween.

For years after that, I thought Devil's Night was nothing more than a plot device—a creation of J. O'Barr for his tale of loss and revenge, later adopted by the iconic film with Brandon Lee. Much later, through, of all places, the autobiography of Violent J from the Insane Clown Posse, I learned that Devil's Night was a real thing. This blew me away.

The reality of Devil's Night elicited a visceral response in me. I was reminded of living just outside of L.A. during the Rodney King Riots and watching dark smoke cloud over the city. Memories of wondering if my father would be dragged out of his car like that truck driver on TV (Reginald Denny) came rushing back with the same emotional impact. I remembered the anger and hatred I saw in the faces on the news—the frustration and misplaced violence—and I couldn't imagine that type of madness happening every year in an American city. I couldn't imagine it being a tradition.

Introduction

But it was a tradition. Every year, from the mid-'70s into the '90s, Detroit would erupt into flame and chaos on the night before Halloween. Bored and destitute kids would set cars on fire for kicks, while angry parents burned down crack houses and gang dens. Career arsonists would pull insurance jobs and opportunists would loot and destroy local businesses.

Maybe Devil's Night was a pressure release for a city about to blow. Perhaps it was a way for people to cope with the racial and economic tensions they were faced with. Or maybe it was something deeper … an ancient and malevolent force lurking in the shadows and the very soil.

Detroit is said to have plenty of demons and bogeymen one could pin Devil's Night on. The Nain Rouge (French for "red dwarf"), the hobgoblin of Michigan, is said to have brought ill tidings going back before the first Europeans set foot on the continent. Legends abound about malevolent ghosts, all the way from the Fox Indian Massacre, up through schoolyard stories of undead pig-faced butchers. The specter of Henry Ford and the echoes of his bigotry still loom over the city, and countless lives are sacrificed each year to the demon kings of crack and heroin.

What if the specters of Motor City were real, in a truly literal sense? What if they had poisoned the land, the water, and the very soul of the city with their negativity? These are the questions I sought to explore in this collection.

To quote the 1948 film *The Naked City,* "this is a story of a number of people and also a story of the city itself." Inspired as much by the work of Frank Miller and J. O'Barr as by Machen, Lovecraft, Barker, and Carpenter, *Devil's Night* is a tour through the myths, personalities and the collective spirit of a haunted place during a troubled time.

The research for this book was intense. I studied maps, scoured old newspapers, and read several books about the history and folklore of Detroit. I sought out locals and consulted people who witnessed more than a few Devil's Nights firsthand. I watched interviews with gang members and drug dealers, police and politicians. I read up on every Michigan-related urban legend on the internet and listened to word-of-mouth accounts of more obscure legends. It is my hope that I've captured the atmosphere in a genuine way and that I treated the history, culture, and folklore of Detroit with frankness and all due respect.

So now I ask you to join me on this strange night of orange flame and black magic—a time when the veil between worlds is thin and madness descends on man like a plague. I invite you to walk with me, through the cold October chill and the warmth of a hundred burning buildings. I challenge you to look upon the terrors lurking in condemned buildings and those lying in wait beneath the Detroit River.

Fire it up! Fire it up!

Curtis M. Lawson
Salem, Massachusetts
July 2020

Detroit, Michigan
October 30th, 1987 …

Trash-Fire Stories

Atomized paint hissed from an aerosol can, marking the concrete wall with streaks of black. The fumes from the spray paint made Clyde dizzy, despite the bandana covering his nose and mouth. While the sensation wasn't entirely unpleasant, he feared he might fall from his ladder. He turned his head away from the mural he was painting, pulled the bandana down from his face, and took a deep breath. The room still spun around him, but that sense of vertigo diminished.

Clyde decided that it was time for a break. He climbed down the steps of the old aluminum ladder and backed away to look at his work in progress. Curled red lips were painted around a frame that once housed double doors, and jagged teeth loomed above, turning the egress into a wicked mouth.

The mural was nearly done, or maybe it was done. Clyde always had a hard time deciding if something was finished. The sketches in his notebooks were constantly evolving things, many having peaked long ago, then ruined by the burden of added pencil marks and ink strokes. Others had become completely different drawings from what they started as, the original lines forgotten in a long history of erasing and adjusting.

It didn't help matters that the light in the abandoned auto factory was shit. The power had been cut off long ago, so the only illumination came from a trashcan fire Clyde had lit when he got there. A bit of dusk's fading light penetrated through windows high above the factory floor, but the oncoming night was quickly devouring that illumination.

Clyde eyed the mural, a massive and hideous face that encompassed a passageway to some dark, crumbling part of the abandoned factory. He looked for signs of asymmetry between the coal-black eyes and the long, hooked nose. He sought out black drips where the creature's hair and patchy beard met its crimson skin. He examined his shading and highlights, making sure they lined up with the imaginary light source in his mind. There were mistakes and problem areas. Not many, but enough that he couldn't call the piece finished.

"Shit! That is dope, son!"

Clyde turned with a start. He'd been so focused on his art that he hadn't heard anyone come into the factory. What he found upon turning was a boy about his own age, fifteen or so, dressed in an oversized camo jacket and black cargo pants; he had a backpack slung across one shoulder. His name was Nick Diggs, and Clyde kind of knew him from school.

"You scared me," Clyde said with a nervous laugh.

"That's 'cause you're creeping yourself out with that heavy-metal demon shit you be painting there."

Clyde let out a small laugh, then shifted the spray can back and forth between his hands.

"So … what are you doing here?" Clyde asked after a few moments of silence.

Before Nick could answer, the sound of hard wheels on concrete echoed from another part of the factory, closer to the entrance. A girl with short red pigtails came into view through the doorway. She was riding a skateboard, and a chubby Arab kid in a Ramones T-shirt was rushing to keep up. They were also kids from Clyde's school—Shelby Lieber and Muhammed Barati.

"Oh shit, dude! That is sick!" the girl exclaimed as she tried, and failed, to ollie the threshold. "What is it, like the devil?"

"No," Clyde said, hanging his head down. "It's the Nain Rouge."

"The hobgoblin of Michigan, motherfucker!" Nick yelled, before going into a freestyle rap. "Straight outta Detroit like the Nain Rouge, spinning tracks, like I was a centrifuge."

Muhammed started beatboxing, urging Nick to keep going. Shelby rolled her eyes and walked over to the trashcan fire. She held her hands up to its warm glow.

"I think we have algebra together. Clyde, right?" she asked. Clyde nodded and mumbled something akin to *yes*.

"Is all this yours?" Shelby asked, gesturing to the graffiti that covered every wall and much of the floor.

"Some of it. Not the crummy little tags; I don't really mess with that bullshit. All the more elaborate stuff is me, though," Clyde said, pointing toward portraits of superheroes and movie killers. "I make street art—murals and shit like that."

The two boys joined Shelby by the flaming trashcan and took a moment to appreciate the artwork that surrounded them. Clyde tossed his spray can to the ground and joined them by the fire.

"So what y'all doing here? And on Devil's Night?"

"We thought we'd drink a few beers and smoke a little weed," Shelby replied. "Just kind of a low-key party. That cool with you, or are we gonna fuck up your artistic vibe?"

"No, that's cool. You got an extra beer?"

Nick smiled and retrieved a six-pack of Old Milwaukee from his backpack. He broke four of the beers free from their plastic rings and handed them out. Clyde cracked his open and took a swig. The cold, hoppy carbonation helped drive away the paint-fume fog in his head.

"You know, I saw the Nain Rouge once," Muhammed said, admiring the demonic face on the concrete wall.

"Shit, I seen that little red bastard today," Nick replied. Shelby let out a huff and a laugh that rang with skepticism.

"It's true, yo. You know them kids who be dealing that china white over by East Warren? They all ran up in one of them little raghead stores …" Nick turned toward Muhammed and cocked his head in a sort of non-apology. "No offense," he muttered.

Muhammed shrugged and took a sip from his beer.

"Like I said, them kids from East Warren all just rushed this store, so I followed them in. We all started snatching shit up, which is how I got these beers. But then the owner comes out from behind the counter, waving a hand cannon, so we all rush out before the crazy motherfucker can shoot one of us."

"What the hell does this have to do with the Nain Rouge, Nick?" Shelby asked.

"I'm getting to it!" he said. "So I get out to the street and I see one of them little gangbanger kids get pistol-whipped and dragged back into the store. And who's standing across the street watching the whole thing with a smile on his face? Some red-skinned little dwarf motherfucker."

Shelby snorted and almost choked on her beer. She shook her head and pawed at her nose, which burned from the carbonation. "Or you just saw a kid in a Halloween costume, you dumbass."

"Halloween ain't 'til tomorrow, and I know what I saw! I bet that Arab dude chopped that little gangster to bits in his basement. Like some *Texas Chainsaw 2* shit, but with curry instead of chili. That's the kind of business that goes down when the Nain Rouge shows up. He's like a bad omen!"

"Man, curry ain't even Arab," Muhammed said, shaking his head.

Clyde stuffed a can of red spray paint into the pocket of his sweatshirt and climbed back up the ladder, still holding his beer. He set the can of Old Milwaukee on top of the ladder, pulled his bandana back up over his face, then retrieved the spray can from his pocket. The ball bearing inside the can clicked against the aluminum as he shook the paint. It was a sound that Clyde found solace in. Once the paint was properly agitated he went about the careful work of touching up the black drips on the hairline of his rendered monster.

"You said you saw him, too?" Clyde asked, looking over his shoulder at Muhammed. "The Nain Rouge, I mean?"

"I did. But the Nain Rouge isn't some little red dwarf … or at least that's not how I saw it."

"What the hell does that mean?" Shelby asked.

"So my grandfather, my mom's dad, he lives on the Isabella Indian Reservation. He's really into that old medicine-man shit. My dad doesn't like me around him, he says all that native spirituality is satanic bullshit in disguise, but my mom insists I spend a week with him every summer on the reservation."

"I thought you were a dot Indian, not a feather one," Nick said.

"Man, you're an asshole. My dad's from Iran, and my mom is Native American."

Nick rolled his eyes and took a sip from his beer. "Whatever. Just tell your damn story."

"So it was late in August, two summers ago, and Gramps takes me out camping on some reservation land. He's trying to teach me about plants and animals and shit, when we come to this giant pile of rocks. They were all this ruddy orange color, more like dried blood than rust. Dark purple vines with sharp-looking leaves clung to the stones, wrapping all around and in between them.

"I went over to check out the mound and Gramps pulled me back, telling me that an angry spirit lived in the rocks and that I'd get its attention if I touched it. He said that's what the first White men did when they came here, thinking these stones were this color because they were rich with iron, when really they wept blood.

"That's why Detroit became such a powerful city, but also why it's always been corrupt—because the White men stole the power from these rock spirits. And when the spirits appeared and demanded something in return, the White men could only perceive them in a way they understood—fairy tales and hobgoblins—which took form as the Nain Rouge. Since they mistook the spirits for monsters, they never made the proper sacrifices, so the spirits cursed the city with anger and sickness. They poisoned the water and cursed the soil with hate and violence, and the curse grew over time until the city started to burn once a year when the veil between the physical and spirit worlds is at the weakest."

"And you believed that shit?" Shelby asked.

"Not at first, but later that night I saw it for myself. We camped a bit away from that rock formation, but around dusk I went off on my own to gather firewood or whatever, and I decided to go back to the rocks. I wanted to see if I could—I don't know—if I could feel anything. I decided that the pile of rocks did kind of look like a sleeping giant, if you looked at it just right, especially in the dying sunset. I could make out these massive limbs and a creepy, misshapen head. There were even these indents filled with heavy shadows that looked like jet-black eyes.

"What really freaked me out, though, was how quiet it was around the stones. There we no birds chirping or squirrels chattering. Not even the sound of crickets. It was just dead silent.

"And then I noticed all the other plants in the area, everything but those vines that grew across and between the rocks were all sick and wilting. Even the trees nearby were leafless and decrepit. It was like the rock formation was leeching evil and death into the ground, just like my grandfather said, or maybe it was sucking the life out from everything else.

"Still, I was curious, so I reached out and pressed my hand against the stones—just what Gramps had warned me against. The vines came to life when I touched the rocks, and they slithered toward my fingertips. The whole pile of stones trembled and growled, then they shifted and moved. It was like the vines were muscles and tendons and the rocks were bone."

"Bullshit," Shelby said.

"No bullshit. And it got even crazier. The rocks, all bound up together by those purple vines, they stood up like a person. It kind of looked like that rock dude from the Fantastic Four, but like a nightmare version. It reached out for me, its stone fist crawling with thorny vines that dripped black venom.

"The thing swatted at me, but I stumbled back and fell on my ass, so it just missed. If I hadn't been a klutz it would have caved my head in, or at least shredded my face with those nasty, dripping thorns. As soon as I hit the ground I scrambled off into the woods as fast as I could. I don't know if it tried to follow me. I didn't look back until I got back to our camp, and by then there was no sign of it."

"Were you on mushrooms when you saw this?" Nick asked.

"Man, that's not the point, all right?"

Nick and Shelby broke into howling laughter. Clyde snickered beneath the bandana that covered his face as he sprayed short bursts of paint close to the wall.

"Trippy spirit visions and trick-or-treaters," Shelby said shaking her head. "You guys are regular Ghostbusters!"

Nick was now crouched on the floor, rolling a joint on the dirty concrete. He looked up at her with a smirk. "You got a better Nain Rouge story, Shelby?"

The three boys looked toward Shelby. She stood quiet for a moment, then took a long sip from her beer.

"Do I?" she asked, turning to stare into the flames of the trash fire. Her face was cold and blank, save for the reflection of the flames in her eyes.

"One year on Devil's Night a young girl went out to an abandoned building to drink with her friends." Her voice was low, her words careful and measured. "A building just like this …"

She closed her eyes and took a deep breath. The beer can shook in her hand and tears welled up in her eyes.

Nick was captivated by her intensity and fumbled to light his joint.

"God, all she wanted was a good time. She just wanted to laugh and party a little, but that didn't happen. No, something terrible and unspeakable went down instead."

Shelby stopped talking and continued staring into the fire. Tears were slowly running down her cheeks, and her lower lip trembled. The three boys watched her, rapt in sudden fear and sadness.

"What happened?" Muhammed asked.

"She died. Her friends—they …" She sniffed and lowered her head. Her hand came up to cover her eyes as she cried. "They literally bored her to death with bullshit urban legends."

Shelby lifted her head, crocodile tears still running down her cheeks, but a wide smile stretched across her lips. She stuck her tongue out and raised a middle finger to her friends.

"Oh, fuck you," Muhammed said, throwing his empty beer can at her.

Clyde climbed down the ladder and swapped out the red spray paint for a can of orange. He shook it, staring at his mural and considering what sections might still need some highlights.

"What about you, Rembrandt?" Nick asked. "You ever see the Nain Rouge?"

"I have," Clyde said. He kept his eyes fixed on the mural of the aforementioned creature, not bothering to turn and look at Nick as he answered. "Every Devil's Night for four years, in fact."

He sprayed a quick arc of orange paint along the sharp bridge of the Nain Rouge's nose, then took a step back. After a moment of considering his imaginary light source, he flicked his wrist and gave the nozzle a quick push, adding some lighting to the ridge of the creature's left nostril.

"The first time, I was out with my older brother, Matt. He was fifteen and I was only twelve, but I begged him to let me come out with him and his friends. He said I could if I did his chores for a week, and of course I said I would.

"We started off the night just doing stupid shit. Egging cars. Smearing Vaseline on payphones. Tagging up buildings. Some of the kids smashed some pumpkins and I remember that making me mad-sad. I drew a lot, even back then, and I remember thinking how much work someone put into carving those Jack-o'-Lanterns, and how shitty it was just to come and break them. I didn't dare say shit to my brother's friends, though. I mean, I was twelve and they were letting me hang out and raise hell with them.

"As the night went on and things escalated we ended up down by these train tracks. Everyone was drinking and playing around on the rails. Matt gave me my first beer that night. I thought I was such a badass, but then I saw this thing in the woods behind the tracks and it just sucked the breath from my lungs. It looked like a cartoon devil—deep red skin over wiry muscles and a patchy black beard on its face. It was short and stout and butt-ass naked.

"The woods around the thing moved with a life of their own.

Vines writhed along the ground and up the monster's carnelian flesh. Tree roots broke free from the soil and stretched toward me like the tentacles of something in a bad monster movie. All the while the Nain Rouge just stared at me with these eyes that were so intensely black—like blacker than the night.

"The thing licked its lips with a barbed, purple tongue that was split down the middle. It glared at me and held me in that empty gaze. The rest of the world was pushed into the background as it held my mind captive with those lifeless eyes. I vaguely remember hearing the cheers and screams from Matt and his friends. I kind of recall the sound of the oncoming train, then the gust of wind as it passed.

"It wasn't until the Nain Rouge broke its gaze and retreated into the tree line that I realized what had happened. People were crying and screaming behind me. I could hear someone puking, and God-awful smells flooded my senses—blood and shit and vomit. When I turned I saw my brother on the ground ... or what was left of him. His chest on up lay in the gravel, his flesh already ashy from the enormous blood loss. Some of his remains were on the tracks—a bloody mess of ruined flesh and shredded clothing. The rest of him got carried off with the train."

Shelby, Nick, and Muhammed were silent. Clyde was still focused on his mural, and his back was turned to them as he considered which of the spray cans he wanted to use next. The three friends looked at one another, each hoping for some cue as to how they should react.

"Shit, man ..." Nick began but didn't finish.

"It is what it is," Clyde said, opting for a can of gray so he could tweak his shading.

"What about the other three times?" Muhammed asked. Shelby backhanded him in the chest and gave him a dirty look. He let out a muffled huff and rubbed his chest.

Clyde looked back at the three friends, a sad smile on his face. "No, it's cool. I don't mind talking about it."

He turned back to the mural, adding a dusting of gray shading here and there. The monster had looked impressive when Shelby, Nick, and Muhammed had first got here, but now it almost looked alive. Shelby looked into the black-painted eyes of the Nain Rouge and thought about Clyde's story—how that gaze held him in place. A cold sensation ran through her blood and bones, forcing her to look away.

"The second time I saw the Nain Rouge was exactly one year after my brother died. I didn't go out that Devil's Night, even though I had friends of my own that were out causing trouble. My mom wouldn't let me, not after what happened to Matt, especially with all the fires and shit getting worse each year. Honestly, I didn't want to anyway.

"Instead I stayed home and drew creepy shit in my sketchbook, mainly the Nain Rouge, while watching Count Scary host some corny monster flick. The reception got all shitty, and the picture cut out halfway through. I screwed with the rabbit ears and banged on the side of the set, but it stayed all static, so I shut it off.

"As the screen went black I could see it reflected in the glass of the TV set—the Nain Rouge standing right behind my couch. I froze and watched it on the screen. The monster opened its mouth and that awful tongue wriggled past its jagged teeth. Its black-hole eyes stared at me from the glass, threatening to hold me in place and hypnotize me again, but I wasn't having it.

"I spun around, ready to jab my pen into that fucking devil's throat, but there was nothing there. I got up and checked behind the couch, but I was alone in the room. When I looked back at the TV, the Nain Rouge was still reflected in the glass, licking at the air and staring me down.

"I pissed myself a little. I'm not even ashamed to say it. I was that damn scared. I didn't wait for the thing to disappear on its own this time. I ran screaming into my mom's room. I didn't even bother to knock, which would usually end up with me getting an ass-whooping, but I didn't care.

"There was no ass-whooping, though, and no help to be found. I thought she was asleep at first, but she wouldn't wake up, no matter how hard I tried shaking her or how loud I screamed. That's when I realized she wasn't breathing. On her nightstand was a picture of Matt, wet with her tears, next to an empty pill bottle and a glass of cheap wine."

"Jesus Christ," Shelby muttered. "I'm so sorry, dude."

Clyde shrugged and continued shading minute details on his mural. The others looked at the monstrous image with new eyes. The sharp nose and cheekbones. The jagged teeth like broken shards of ivory. Those intensely empty eyes. It looked less cartoonish now, not some heavy metal album cover, but a genuine image of evil.

"After my mom died I moved in with my Uncle Horace. He was a good dude—a studio musician with a love of art. He made a decent living playing piano and keys on a bunch of other people's records. He even did some work for Berry Gordy. Since he had some cash and didn't work regular hours, he made it a point to take me out to museums and concerts, which was something new for me.

"He owned his own house out in the suburbs, which was nicer than any place I'd ever lived. A big yard and cable TV. The whole nine yards. I felt fucking rich, you know? More importantly it was out past Eight Mile, and beyond the city limits. As October approached I figured I was safe. I was out of Detroit, away from Devil's Night and the Nain Rouge. I was wrong, though.

"I was walking home from school on the day before Halloween when I saw the Nain Rouge again. This time wasn't like the others, maybe because I was out in the suburbs, but it was just as scary. Maybe even more so because my guard was down.

"There was a devil mask, one of those cheap plastic jobs you get at the drug store, and it was nailed to a tree near our house. My blood ran cold when I saw it, but I tried to tell myself it was just some bullshit Halloween decoration. I took a deep breath, shook out my limbs to try to cast out my fear, and walked over to the tree with the mask on it.

"Sap congealed around the nail that punctured the forehead of the mask and held it to the tree. Black moss extended from the bark of the tree, up the plastic mask, forming an inconsistent beard. A dark, thorny vine was wrapped around the trunk and it jutted out from the mouth of the mask. Two purple leaves with jagged edges split off from the vine, like the forked tongue of the Nain Rouge.

"I looked into the eyes of the mask, and I should have seen brown bark behind them, but all I saw was a gaping, black emptiness. I even jabbed my finger into one of the eyeholes, and as deep as I probed I couldn't feel the tree. Just the same terrible, cold nothingess I had seen in the eyes of the Nain Rouge on the nights my brother and my mother died.

"I ran home and found the front door locked. I still remember fumbling with my keys and dropping them like some chump in a horror movie. When I got the door open, I stumbled in screaming for Uncle Horace, but he didn't answer. There was a plate of Oreos and a ham sandwich on the table, next to a folded note.

"The note was from Uncle Horace, and it said he got a call from some studio in the city after I went to school. Another piano player flaked out and they wanted him to lay down a few tracks. If I had been home when he got the call I would have begged him to stay. I would have cried and screamed and done anything to keep him from going into the city. I wasn't home, though, and he went to the studio … he went into the city.

"That was a year ago, today. Uncle Horrace never came home, which you probably guessed. He got caught in the crossfire of some drug deal gone wrong and I never saw him again.

"And I think it's done …" Clyde said, switching gears in an abrupt manner. He grabbed his beer off the ladder stepped back to where the others stood and eyed his massive depiction of the Nain Rouge's face. His lips curled into the slightest trace of a smile. Satisfied, he placed the can of Krylon to the floor.

"Wait, are you fucking with us?" Shelby asked. "You really lost three family members, one Devil's Night after the next?"

"Yeah." Clyde nodded. "I'm not the only one, either. I've heard similar stories from other people."

He was still staring at the mural, a vacant expression on his face. His gaze was locked with the black discs that were the eyes of the monstrous painting.

"I told you!" Nick exclaimed, a trail of marijuana smoke following his words. "That little red bastard is like a bad omen. You see that motherfucker and you know some bad shit is gonna go down!"

"You said you saw him four times," Shelby prodded, her skepticism shining through. "That's only three."

"The fourth time is tonight, right now," Clyde said, pointing toward the mural he had just painted around the dark passageway.

"I don't have any family left. I've lost touch with all the friends I ever had. I don't even get along with anyone at the group home I'm in, so I thought it would come for me this year. I figured if that was the case I'd at least see the thing on my own terms, so I painted the motherfucker here, where he couldn't run off or vanish. I wanted to look him in the face as I died."

Nick looked to Shelby, then both of them looked to Muhammed. None of the kids knew what to say, and the absolutism of Clyde's tone made them all uneasy.

"Whatever happened these last few years, that was just a terrible coincidence. You're not gonna die tonight," Shelby said, placing a hand on Clyde's shoulder.

"I know," Clyde said, tears pooling in his eyes. "I was supposed to, though. But then you three showed up. You shared your beer and your stories. You all listened to mine."

Clyde began to cry silently, unashamed of his tears and unwilling to hide them. The whole time he talked his eyes were focused on the painting he had just created.

"And now it's almost like we're friends."

The three other teens were as focused on Clyde as he was on his art, so none of them saw the tangled vines snake out from the darkness beyond the double doorway, like some horrible barbed tongue. They didn't hear the soft scraping of the thorns across the concrete or note the trails of black venom secreted in their wake.

Nick was the first to realize that something was wrong. The vines wrapped around his ankle and pulled his legs out from under him. The vines constricted around his ankle, the thorns shredding the skin beneath his pant leg and pumping venom into his bloodstream. He screamed, but the sound was cut short as his face slammed into the filthy, concrete floor.

Shelby and Muhammed jumped back and issued their own cries of alarm. The vines were dragging Nick back toward the space beyond the darkened threshold that served as the mouth of the Nain Rouge mural. He clawed at the filthy concrete, scraping up his palms and breaking his fingernails.

Shelby dived forward, grabbing Nick's hand and struggled to pull him back. She grunted and cried for help. The screams of his friends snapped Muhammed out of his fear-born paralysis and he rushed forward to grab Nick's other hand. As they played tug of war with his body, the vines constricted and lacerated the flesh around Nick's ankle. An ugly, pained cry escaped his lips.

The tangle of vines split apart, and this new branch lunged out at Shelby. It coiled around her wrist and climbed up her forearm, flaying the skin as it went. The pain was too much. She lost her grip on Nick and collapsed onto her chest.

Muhammed dug his feet against the ground and pulled on Nick with all his might. Whatever was dragging them into the darkness—whatever was pulling them into the mouth of that hideous painting—it was stronger than Muhammed. Black trails of rubber formed on the floor where his sneakers skidded across the rough concrete.

The vines that had wrapped around Nick's ankle now worked their way up his body, stripping flesh from bone. Eventually they encircled his arm, then grasped onto Muhammed. He howled in pain and fear as the first of the thorns bit into the back of his hand.

Realizing that the thing now had him as well, Muhammed glanced back at Clyde with a look of desperation. He reached out with one hand and begged for help.

Clyde simply stood there weeping, staring into the eyes of the Nain Rouge painted on the wall as it devoured his three new friends.

D20

Andre looked out the window, admiring the smoky orange hue that the burning city lent to the night sky. He didn't like the idea that people were getting hurt, or that bad guys were robbing and stealing, but he found a kind of beauty in Devil's Night. The city was ugly, pretty much year-round. In summer it smelled like hot trash and motor oil, the streets littered with cigarette butts and Miller cans. In the winter it was blanketed in gray-brown slush and colorless ice. But on Devil's Night the Detroit sky burned like an autumn-colored aurora.

David wrestled with the rabbit ears on the TV, while his little brother stared out the window. Count Scary was hosting an airing of *Halloween* on Channel 4, and he figured their mom wouldn't notice or care if they watched it. It was a Friday night, so there was no school in the morning. More importantly, she was tweaking out at the kitchen table, waiting for her scumbag boyfriend to show up with some dope to share.

Michael Myers took shape on the Magnavox, barely visible under a fog of television static. David tweaked the antennas a bit more, and the movie was lost beneath a field of shifting black and white sand.

"Damn it," he said, slapping the side of the TV.

"It ain't gonna work," Andre said, his eyes still focused out the window and on the hazy amber skyline.

"It usually comes in just fine," David replied, still fussing with the TV. "Probably all the damn smoke and fire interfering with the signal."

"I don't think that's how TV signals work."

"What do you know about how TVs work? You're twelve."

A loud knock came at the apartment door. Andre and David both swallowed hard and looked over to the door, then to each other. A cold shiver ran down their spines in unison.

"Open up, Wendy! It's the candyman!"

That deep, ugly voice—it reminded David of gravel and gasoline. Both boys hated the sound of that voice.

The door shuddered in its frame as the person outside beat on it with growing impatience. Their mother shambled from the kitchen, a cigarette hanging from her lips. She smoothed out her dress and quickly fixed her hair before unlocking the deadbolt and the chain lock.

Their mother opened the door and greeted her boyfriend/dope hookup with a kiss on the lips. He turned it into more, grabbing her by the ass and shoving his tongue down her throat. Andre turned away from the sight, looking back out the window. David watched in disgust.

Wolf—that's what their mother's boyfriend called himself—was a tall, gangly biker dude with thin blond hair that hung in long, oily strands. He had a sunken face with long, angular features, like some cartoon villain, and his blue-grey eyes were cold, lifeless voids. His hands were always dirty, with grime ever-present under fingernails that were too long.

Wolf crossed the threshold of the apartment, invading their home. He smirked at David and nodded.

"How's it going, you little shits?"

"Hey," David said, looking down at the floor, before pretending to mess with the rabbit ears again.

Wolf sauntered into the living room, making his presence impossible to ignore. He pushed past David and stood by Andre at the window. Andre shuddered as the nasty biker placed his filthy hand on his shoulder, joining him for a look at the city.

"No need to be scared of the Devil's Night, kid. I got a prospect outside watching my bike. No one's gonna fuck with your house with one of my boys out front."

"I'm not afraid," Andre said without looking over at Wolf.

Wolf patted Andre on the back. The boy flinched, and Wolf laughed, telling him not to be a pussy, then the biker walked back over to the boys' mother and took her by the hand. He smiled as she urged him in the direction of her bedroom.

"I knocked over one of those young boys and got some of that good china white shit," he said, not bothering to whisper. "But you gotta work for it, lady."

She laughed, assuring Wolf that she would. David felt bile rise in his throat.

"You boys may want to turn on some music or some shit," Wolf called out over his shoulder. "I think it's gonna get loud in here."

Their mother playfully smacked Wolf and the two of them went into her room, closing the door behind them.

"Gross," Andre muttered. "I don't want to hear them."

David looked at the TV. Count Spooky, dressed up in his corny signature vampire getup, was barely visible behind the static. His half-ass Bella Lugosi accent cut in and out, like a dying walkie-talkie. David shut off the TV.

"Come on, I have something better we can do."

The boys went to their bedroom and closed the door. It was a small room for two boys to share, but they had bunk beds to maximize space, and they made the best of it. The walls were lined with Andre's crayon drawings and torn-out pages of sci-fi, horror and hip-hop magazines. A stack of comics sat on their shared dresser next to a pile of second-hand board games.

David put a cassette into their boombox, a dubbed copy of a Fat Boys record, and turned up the volume enough to block out whatever Wolf and their mother were up to. Andre did a dumb little dance to the beat while David got together some loose paper, a few books, and a little purple sack with a drawstring.

David plopped himself on the floor and Andre followed suit. He dropped the stack of books and paper in front of him. The one on top featured a demonic statue on the cover and was entitled *Player's Handbook.*

"Man, I don't want to play your nerdy math game," Andre said, rolling his eyes.

"But this isn't going to be just any old adventure. This is a special Devil's Night adventure."

David reached into his pouch and retrieved a crimson twenty-sided die, marbleized with veins of obsidian. He held it in a dramatic fashion, expressing all the flair that came naturally to young dungeon masters.

"This isn't any normal die, Andre. This was given to me by the Nain Rouge himself, last Halloween."

"That's some bullshit," Andre said. "The Nain Rouge ain't real, and I was with you last Halloween, dumbass."

"You don't know what I do when your little ass goes to sleep. I snuck back out and hit up Gray Street."

"Uh-huh," Andre said, his skepticism plain on his young face.

"And you know that empty lot down on the corner of Gray and East Forest?"

"Yeah."

"Well, it wasn't an empty lot. There was a house there, or the ghost of a house—a three-floor Colonial going back to before the big fire in 1805. I knocked on the door and this little midget-looking guy with red skin and a black beard answered the door. I was nervous, but I held out my bag, and he just poofed this twenty-sided die into existence."

David tried to roll the die across his knuckles, like some street magician, but he fumbled it and caught it in his other hand. Both boys laughed, but David fought back his smile and quickly returned to his best impression of stoicism.

"So you're telling me that some ghost house popped up on Gray Street, and you just marched up the steps and held out your trick-or-treat bag to a little goblin man?"

"The Nain Rouge is a hobgoblin, but yeah, that's how it happened. And he gave me the die as a reward for my bravery. He said it was magical and that if I saved it for a very special adventure, my players and I would be rewarded with a treasure beyond compare!"

"You corny, bro.... Can I see it?"

David handed the die to Andre. It felt like stone, rather than the acrylic that most of David's weird dice were made from, and it was warm in Andre's palm. The red veins almost glowed, and the streaks of black were so dark that they looked like empty space. He closed his hand around the die. It made him feel powerful and safe.

"All right. Show me how to play."

⁂

"Many years ago the evil warlord Ulf invaded the sacred city of Bergeron. Ulf's Viking army laid scourge to the city and took over the castle. They enslaved the good citizens of Bergeron and kept them weak and passive with magic and poisonous tinctures. Worst of all, Ulf used his dark magic to cloud the heart and mind of Queen Gwendolyn—the most beautiful and pure-hearted woman in the land—and make her his servant.

"As prince of Bergeron you tried to stop the evil raiders, leading the sacred city's militia, but your combined strength was not enough, and Ulf's men slaughtered you, one and all. But your love for your city and your mother, the queen, was too strong for even death to contain. Your soul traversed the nine realms until you entered the court of the fire giant, Surtr."

"Court? Is he like a judge?"

"Not like a court court. Like a ... a throne room."

David opened a book entitled *Deities and Demigods* and pointed to the entry about Surtr, the fire giant and lord of Muspellheim. A black-and-white line drawing depicted an armored warrior with a beard and hair of flames. The giant held a massive flaming sword that stretched past the borders of the picture.

"Surtr, while a terrible god in his own right, is also an enemy of the Vikings. Because you share an enemy, Surtr has agreed to help you—to give you the power to take back Bergeron and to cleanse the dark magic entrapping your people. In return, you will be his cleric—that's like a priest—and every life you take will be a sacrifice to him."

"Man, I don't wanna play a priest."

"This is a warrior priest, not like Reverend Michael giving sermons down at First Baptist. You'll be armed with a magic sword and an arsenal of fire magic. You'll be protected by mithril plate mail, scorched black by the flames of Muspellheim. But you have to agree to Surtr's terms. He holds out a necklace—a stone polyhedron, red as hate and riddled with veins of blackest night."

David held out the die to his little brother, acting out Surtr's offering. "Do you accept? Will you become Surtr's cleric?"

Andre snatched the die from his brother's hand and smirked. "Hell yeah, I accept!"

"You slip the necklace over your head and the power of Surtr flows through your soul like a surge of magma. Your skin blackens and chars, and your hair ignites. Ancient prayers and invocations burn themselves into your mind. Black-skinned dwarves attend you, fitting you with the scorched armor of Muspellheim, and a great blazing sword, as long as you are tall, materializes in your hands.

"The power I grant you is no toy, Andre of Bergeron," David said, imitating the growl of the fire giant. "Nor is it limitless. Use it wisely, with respect and prudence."

"Dude turns me into a magic flamethrower and tells me not to get stupid with it?"

"Do you say that?"

"What? No, I don't say that to the big-ass fire giant."

"Good. Now look at your sheet."

David went through each cleric spell on Andre's list, as well as the special abilities associated with his weapons and armor. He explained what the numbers meant—how many times he could use each power, how much damage they caused or negated, what kind of range they could be used from. A huge grin crossed his face as his little brother got more excited with each spell. *Inflict Minor Wounds. Flame Strike. Flamewalk. Summon Monster.*

"What's with the *cure light wounds* and *remove curse* shit? I just wanna burn me some Vikings."

"You don't think you'll take any damage from your enemies?"

"Do you see how powerful I am?" Andre asked, holding up his character sheet.

"Never underestimate your enemies, Andre of Bergeron."

"Whatever. What happens next?"

"You step through a blazing portal of wavering orange and find yourself transported back to the city of Bergeron. You appear in the temple of a Viking war god, but your very touch scorches and ignites the wooden floor, setting the invaders' temple alight."

❧

Knox's vision was blurred from staring at numbers for too long. He took off his bifocals, which he would never wear around other members of the club, and rubbed away the fatigue. He didn't need to play catch-up with the books, and the club's finances were well in order, but what the hell else was he going to do on Devil's Night? He was too old to be riding around raising hell with the younger guys, and the Clubhouse was honestly a lot safer and quieter than most of Detroit tonight.

The Clubhouse was empty and that was an added benefit. The prospects and the soldiers were all out running packages and doing some of the higher-risk work that was safer to do while the cops were thinned out dealing with the amateur-hour hooligans of Devil's Night. It was just him in the office, with Mikey and Little Will guarding the door, which meant he was able to focus better than when the place was crawling with coked-out bikers.

He put his bifocals back on and returned his attention to the ledger in front of him. He was currently calculating the interest on people who owed the club outstanding debts and jotting down the names of folks with late payments who needed to be leaned on. His attention was ripped away from his clerical work again as the smoke alarm began to blare.

"What the fuck?" he muttered, getting out of his chair and grabbing his revolver from the desk.

Knox exited the office and stepped into the main hall of the Clubhouse. In the middle of the room, a pillar of orange and yellow fire stretched to the ceiling. Its wavering light reflected off the bottles at the bar, and off the glass of the pinball machines lining one wall. The wooden floor creaked from the heat as flames licked at the rafters above.

The front door burst open, and the two soldiers who had been guarding the door rushed in with pistols drawn. All three men stood dumbfounded as a hellish figure stepped out from the fiery pillar. The creature was in the shape of a man, but its skin was ash and ember. Angry red flame served as the thing's hair, and its eyes were hot coals.

Little Will fired his pistol at the monster. The slug splattered into molten lead on the creature's chest. It turned to the biker who had shot it and pointed a single burning talon at him. It opened its mouth, revealing a tongue of magma and teeth like obsidian arrowheads. The monster growled two words.

༄

"Flame Strike!"

David rolled a D20 for the temple guard, to determine his saving throw. It wasn't the die he had given to Andre, but a solid-color green one made of plain old acrylic. The die stopped on the number six.

"The temple guard does not save! Your *Flame Strike* hits him full force and does—"

David rolled three more dice and totaled up the sum.

"Ten damage! Not quite enough to kill him, but he drops his

weapon and falls to the ground."

"What about system shock?" Andre asked. "You said if I lost half my hit points in a single attack I could die from system shock. What about this guy?"

David looked down at his notes and saw that the temple guards only had fifteen hit points, and since they were humanoid they were susceptible to system shock.

"You're right," he said, rolling two ten-sided dice. "Let's see if he makes it!"

The temple guard, who had a seventy percent chance to survive, rolled poorly, just as he had on his saving throw. David let out a sound of mock sympathy for the NPC and removed the Faygo cap representing him from the grid he'd drawn out on construction paper.

"The first temple guard is overwhelmed by the pain of his burns. He seizes for a brief moment, then goes still. Even in death his skin continues to blister and smoke."

"Now I want to hit this other guy with my flaming sword!"

"Not yet. Now they get to attack!"

⁂

Black smoke wafted up from Little Will's charred corpse. Mikey unloaded his Glock at the monster, screaming and crying as he fired over and over. Knox maintained his cool and rushed for a fire extinguisher. He didn't know what the fuck this thing was, but he'd lived his whole life in Detroit, and it wasn't the first time he'd seen some weird shit.

As a boy, the Nain Rouge had appeared outside his window just before his old man ate a bullet. The Hobo Pig Lady of the East Side had tried to lure him off when he was twelve. He'd been in séances and made love to strippers possessed by dead movie stars. Nothing shook him anymore, not even whatever the hell this was.

The creature ignited the wooden floor with each step it took toward Mikey. It walked with slow, singular purpose, paying no mind to Knox. The old biker took the extinguisher from the wall and snuck up on the monster with a grace that was at odds with his size and demeanor. Once he was a few feet away, Knox unleashed a stream of white mist at the monster's back.

⁂

"The Viking shaman sneaks up behind you and casts cone of cold for sixteen damage."

"You rolled a three and a five!" Andre yelled, pointing at the two dice his brother had just rolled. "That's only eight!"

"Double damage, little bro," David replied. "You're a creature of fire, so you're weak against cold and water attacks."

"Screw these guys. I want to do a spin attack with my big-ass sword. Just swirl around in a circle and cut both these dudes in half."

"Spin attacks aren't a thing. You can't do that."

"You said I could do whatever I wanted in this game," Andre said, frustration in his voice.

David turned to a combat chart in one of the books, ready to explain to his little brother what attacks were acceptable, but stopped when he heard the thudding of his mother's headboard hitting the wall. Both boys went quiet as moans and grunts made their way through the plaster wall separating their bedroom from their mother's.

David stood up and turned the volume louder on the boombox. He looked down at his brother and saw the pain and anger in his eyes—feelings he shared—then sat back down on the floor and closed the book on the combat table.

"Fine, you can try to do a spin attack, but you need to kill the temple guard right out or else your sword will get stuck in him and you won't be able to spin around to hit the shaman."

"I'll kill him in one hit! Don't you worry!"

"Okay, tough guy. Roll the dice."

Andre shook the D20 in his hand, then tossed it to the floor. It landed on a twenty. "That's good, right?"

⁓

The monster lashed out with a red-hot talon and cleaved through Mikey's stomach. His blood and viscera sizzled as it poured from his open belly. The creature followed through with the momentum of its swing, spinning one hundred eighty degrees and driving its scorching claws deep under Knox's ribs.

The old biker screamed out in pain and dropped the fire extinguisher. Blood poured from his mouth, followed by smoke as his insides ignited. The monster turned from Knox's dying form and walked out into the night, leaving the clubhouse to burn away, along with the corpses.

A skyline dotted with flames greeted the monster outside. Sirens blared in every direction, and gangs of angry young men stalked the streets. Some ran away. A few shouted, or threw rocks and bottles. The creature paid them the same heed a man in the jungle might pay swarming flies. With a smooth, deliberate gait, it walked eastward, leaving melted asphalt and scorched concrete in its wake.

⁓

The boombox clicked off as Side A of the cassette ran out of tape. There was no banging, grunting, or moaning coming through the wall anymore, and David assumed that Wolf and his mother had shot up and nodded off already, which meant it should be safe to grab a snack from the kitchen.

"Come on, let's get some chips and Kool-Aid," David suggested.

"I want Faygo."

"It's too late for pop. You'll be up all night."

"You're not the boss of me," Andre argued, puffing out his chest in a way that was as adorable as it was fresh.

Yeah, well, someone needs to raise you, David thought, glaring at the shared wall between their room and their mother's.

David poked his head out of their bedroom to make sure the coast was clear. The living room was empty and their mom's door was still closed. He figured they would be passed out for a while, and he waved for Andre to follow him to the kitchen.

David poured two glasses of cherry Kool-Aid from a plastic pitcher while Andre filled a bowl with chips. As they headed back to their bedroom, loaded up with snacks, David glanced at their mother's door, thinking about how quiet her and Wolf were right now. He wondered if maybe they had OD'd together, and as much as the thought terrified him, part of him wished it to be true. It would hurt if she died—it would kill—but at least it would be over, like tearing off a Band-Aid. It would be better than watching the drugs suck away her life and humanity like an invisible vampire.

"Come on, bro, I got some Viking bitches to kill!" Andre was already in their room, growing impatient as his older brother stood there, lost in thought.

David abandoned his dark musings and smiled at Andre. It made him happy that his brother was getting into the game—that he was able to take his mind off of Wolf and their mom, and the burning city outside.

Back in their bedroom Andre flipped over the Fat Boys tape and hit Play on the boombox while David drew out a new grid and sketched out a few crude landmarks. He placed down bottlecaps and little pink M.U.S.C.L.E. figures around the map to represent different non-player characters and began to lay out a new scene.

"As you march through once-beautiful Bergeron, leaving the bodies of evil men in your wake, you see that the city has fallen into ruin and disarray. A third of the houses are boarded up, abandoned by those lucky enough to escape Viking enslavement. The statues of the benevolent gods have been shattered to make room for the war idols of the invaders.

"The castle stands in the distance—the place you once called home—but it is a dark and twisted reflection of what you remember. Thorny vines climb up the fieldstone walls and heavy clouds bathe it in dark shadows. Its massive gates, once shining gold, have been plundered and replaced with rusty cast iron and rotting timbers."

"That's where I gotta go, right?" Andre asked. "Well, I just burn through the shitty gate and kill this warlord dude."

"Not so fast," David said, pointing out the figures on the map. "A militia has gathered to stop you."

"All right, let's kill them," Andre said, picking up the red-and-black twenty-sided die.

"Wait. These militiamen are not Viking invaders. They are citizens of Bergeron. You even recognize some of them, though they have grown older in the years since your death."

"Then why are they trying to stop me?"

"They don't know you're the prince. Your bargain with Surtr has left you changed, and all they see is a monster. Will you strike them down and prove them right, or will you find another way to get past them?"

⁓

Awestruck firefighters and police surrounded the monster. Citizens on the street fled in terror, while others watched from windows and fire escapes.

A police officer muttered nonsense into his radio, incapable of coming to terms with what he was seeing. A second cop shot at the creature—a futile gesture that was ignored. These men were inconsequential—mere roadblocks.

Two firefighters scrambled to attach a hose to a hydrant. They didn't know what the hell they were looking at, but they knew it was on fire—that it was born of fire. If bullets didn't work, maybe water would.

The monster scanned the area, seeking the path of least resistance. A police car was parked sideways, blocking the street, and two frightened officers were huddled behind it, pointing their weapons.

It held out a glowing finger in the direction of the police cruiser. A single word, *"Move,"* oozed off the creature's magma tongue. Somewhere across the city, a child rolled an unusual die, and the officers, acting out of some will beyond themselves ran off.

The monster blasted the police cruiser with a stream of flame, igniting the gas tank. The car exploded and flew into the air before crashing into a grated storefront. Burning steel and glass showered the street as citizens and first responders scrambled for cover.

Before the creature could make its way through the path it had cleared, an incredible pain tore through its impossible body. It fell to the street, screeching in agony as the firefighters it had ignored assaulted it with a barrage of water.

⁂

"You're running low on hit points," David said with a grave expression.

"Can I use one of my more powerful spells to attack the two wizards?"

"You could, but you would likely kill them, and you know they are good people just trying to protect their home. They aren't Viking invaders."

"Well, shit, what else can I do?"

"Look at your sheet!" David said in a tone that bordered on scolding.

Andre ran his finger down the character sheet, scanning through his spells and abilities, finally stopping on one that looked promising.

"What about *Flamewalk?* It says I can travel between any two fires on the prime material plane."

"Yeah," David said. "That's one of my homebrew abilities. I thought it would be cool for a cleric of Surtr."

"So can I use it?"

"Only if you can reach the fire. You need to be able to actually touch flame in order to *Flamewalk*. You're too far away right now."

Andre looked down at his sheet again, studying his spells and considering his problem. His expression shifted from frustration to pride as he found an answer to his conundrum.

"I cast *Summon Monsters* to create a distraction!"

Fighting through the pain of the barrage of water, the monster shed parts of itself. The clumps of smoldering ash, five in total, hit the ground and morphed into flaming insects the size of cats. The simulacra scattered, attacking the firehose, nearby buildings, and parked cars.

Tiny fires broke out wherever the incendiary bug-things touched. The canopies of bodegas ignited, and trashcans erupted with flame at their touch. One of them burned a hole through the firehose, sacrificing itself to the deluge of water that escaped. It had done its job, though.

The pressure dwindled. Water ceased to flow from the end of the hose and the creature was free from the watery assault. The monster shambled, gasping and steaming, toward the fiery wreckage of the police cruiser. Someone was shooting it in the back, and the heat of the burning lead felt good after the agony of the firehose.

The monster reached out for the flaming car, becoming one with the blaze, then vanished. The insect-things it had left behind crumbled into lifeless ash and ember. The cops and firefighters, and the hustlers and homebodies all stood silent trying to process the sudden calm and what had come just before. The only noise came from crackling flames, the water rushing from the ruined hose, and the sirens in the distance.

"You shift from the elemental plane of fire and back into the prime material plane. You emerge from the hearth in the queen's throne room. She sits chained and ensorcelled …"

"What the hell does *ensorcelled* mean?"

"Like under a spell. She sits chained, under the spell of the Viking warlord Ulf. Her eyes are sunken and lifeless, but something sparks in her gaze when she sees you. It's like she can almost remember you. It's like she can almost remember life before Ulf and his men corrupted the sacred city."

Andre scanned both sides of his character sheet, looking for a spell or attack that might drop the warlord in a single hit. One caught his eye—something fittingly brutal for a Viking warlord.

"I cast—"

"Not so fast. We need to roll initiative to see who goes first."

The brothers rolled their twenty-sided dice in unison.

༄

Wendy was passed out in her bed. Wolf got dressed, fighting hard not to nod off again. He'd love to just pass out naked beside her, but it was Devil's Night and he had a few jobs to run for the club before the night was over.

Wolf fished a glass pipe out of his jacket pocket and packed it with crystal meth from a tiny Ziploc baggie. He needed to even out before he got back on his bike. He couldn't afford to start dozing off and rack up his Harley.

He pulled out a plastic lighter and sparked a flame. The lighter exploded in his hands and hot plastic shrapnel cut into his face and hands. His glass pipe fell from his lips and shattered against the floor as burning butane and ambient heat grew into a creature of ash and flame, almost as tall as himself.

Wolf backed away from the monster and grabbed his pistol off Wendy's nightstand. He thrust it forward as if he were trying to hold back a vampire with a cross. In many ways, it was the closest thing to a holy symbol he knew.

"You ain't real," he muttered. "Just some bad dope. That's all it is, just tainted fucking dope!"

The music from the other room stopped between songs, and he could hear one of Wendy's brats shouting some bullshit about *Boiling Blood,* then a new song started blasting through the wall. The monster locked gazes with Wolf. Hate gleamed in its charcoal eyes, and Wolf felt an incredible heat spread through his body. Steaming blood bubbled out from every orifice. His skin blistered as veins burst beneath. He tried to scream, but his voice was choked by the scolding blood seeping into his lungs. Thrashing about in agony, Wolf crashed through the closed window and out to the concrete sidewalk below.

☙

"Did you hear something?" Andre asked.

"Just ignore it. Trust me," David said, having grown more numb to the drama between his mother and Wolf than his younger brother had.

"Let's finish the adventure," he said, changing the subject back to the game. "The warlord Ulf is an ashen husk at your feet and the queen stares at you. She is afraid and confused, but you think you see a glimmer of hope in her expression as well."

"What am I supposed to do?" Andre asked. "There's nobody left to fight."

"An adventure isn't all about fighting. It's about saving the day and being the hero."

"Well, I already did that, right? I killed the bad guys!"

"But Queen Gwendolyn is still under Ulf's spell, trapped within herself. Nothing you just did matters if you can't help her now."

Andre looked through his stats and powers again. He had ignored his healing magic throughout the entire adventure. It was boring to him, but now he spotted a spell that he thought might save the day and win the adventure.

"I cast *Remove Curse*."

☙

The monster turned to Wendy, who was passed out beneath a thin sheet. It opened its terrible maw, expelling its burning lifeforce past its jagged, obsidian teeth, and into Wendy, through her mouth and nose. The charred body, empty of its power and heat, collapsed into a pile of cinders.

Wendy convulsed on her bed, rivers of sweat running down

her skin, soaking the sheets. She gasped for breath that would not come. Her skin burned and mucus ran freely from her nose. This continued for a minute or so, then her breath came back, her muscles relaxed, and her temperature regulated.

A wave of nausea overcame her. She rolled over, puking onto Wolf's leather jacket, which lay on her floor. When it was done and her stomach settled, she felt good. She felt better than good, in fact. She felt clean and new. The dull, ever-present ache in her gut was gone, and the gnawing addict voice in her skull had gone quiet.

She sat up and looked around the room. The window was destroyed, the glass and the frame completely shattered. Wolf was gone, but his jacket was still there, covered in her vomit. The shattered pieces of his pipe lay in a heap of ash on the floor, next to a necklace that looked like one of the funny dice David liked to play with.

Wendy walked over to the open window and stared outside. Wolf lay smoldering on the filthy sidewalk, an arm's length away from his motorcycle. Some other biker was peeling away on a Harley, leaving Wolf's corpse behind.

Wendy turned back into the room. She grabbed a needle and a bag of china white from her nightstand and threw it out the window, out to Wolf, where it belonged. Dope had no place in her life anymore.

❧

"And with the queen back on her throne and the sacred city of Bergeron restored, Surtr summons you back to Muspellheim," David said, tucking his hand-drawn maps into the *Dungeon Master's Guide*.

"And that's it?"

"For now," David replied. "Did you have fun?"

"Yeah, I guess it was all right, for a geek-boy math game," Andre said, trying to hide his smile. "But I thought you said the Nain Rouge promised you a treasure beyond compare."

Before David could answer a knock came at their door. A second later it opened and their mother stood across the threshold. Her face was streaked with tears, and her skin glistened with sweat, but she looked more beautiful and alive than either could ever remember her.

Devil's Tongue

The rusted bell over the door clanged as Jimmy and a mob of other teens and pre-teens rushed into the store. The Arab shopkeeper yelled at them from behind the bulletproof glass separating his side of the counter from theirs. There were only two children allowed in the store at a time, a measure intended to cut down on shoplifting. The sign on the door said as much, and the shopkeeper repeated it now.

Jimmy and the others ignored his words just as they ignored his sign. They ran down the narrow aisles, most of them pocketing candy bars or gum and snatching comics and music magazines from spinner racks. Jimmy and a few others went straight to the coolers in the back of the store.

Some of the kids howled like animals. Some told the clerk to call the cops, knowing full well the police weren't about to answer a shoplifting call on Devil's Night. Others mocked the shopkeeper with bad impressions of Indian accents as they filled their pockets and backpacks. It didn't matter that the shopkeeper spoke with an Iraqi accent. To the kids, it was all the same.

The shopkeeper reached for the .44 Magnum that sat on the shelf behind him. He made a show of checking the chambers and spinning the cylinder as he made his way to the locked door that separated his side of the counter from the rest of the store.

"Think you can steal from me?" he screamed. "I'll put a hole in each one of you fatherless bastards!"

The shopkeeper unlocked the bulletproof door and stepped out from behind the counter with his Magnum drawn. Some of Jimmy's friends ran for the door, dropping their ill-gotten gains to the ground as they hightailed it. Others pushed their luck, rushing to snag a few more Twinkies or another bag of Big League Chew before they made a break for it.

Jimmy himself kept low and shoved another forty into his backpack. The shopkeeper turned around and caught sight of him zipping up his backpack by the coolers.

"You have some balls on you, you little shit," the shopkeeper said, pointing his gun at Jimmy.

Jimmy cursed, wishing he was packing. Young Boys Inc., the gang he ran with, didn't carry guns, though. Mostly they slung dope, and carrying a piece complicated shit if they got nabbed by the pigs. Besides, they didn't really need guns. They'd driven all the older dealers out of the neighborhood with bats and knives.

The shopkeeper marched toward him, the iron sight of his pistol parked over Jimmy's chest. The boy feigned a dash to the right, then darted to the left, keeping his body low. He rushed in a crouching run for the door, keeping an aisle of product between them.

Jimmy was fast and he outpaced the bulky clerk. He rushed around the endcap of chips and popcorn and toward the exit before the shopkeeper had made it down the aisle.

At the door, he turned with a smirk. "Thank you very much," he said in a bad accent that sounded like a bastardized mix of an Indian caricature and every Middle Eastern movie villain.

It was a stupid, arrogant move, turning around to mock the man, and it gave the shopkeeper the time he needed to catch up. The shopkeeper raised his gun and brought the chrome grip of the pistol down across Jimmy's face.

One of the other boys stopped and turned back to help Jimmy as he fell. The shopkeeper pointed the pistol at this second boy, and after a few seconds of consideration the other little gangbanger ran off without him.

First there was pain—pain on a primal level that pounds and aches, bleeding even into unconsciousness. Then there was thought. *What happened? Where am I?*

Jimmy could only open one of his eyes. The other was swollen shut and maybe worse. It felt like the socket was shattered, and he wondered if he was even in possession of his left eye any longer.

His ass was wet from the damp cement floor. His arms had been pulled back around a metal pole and plastic zip ties bound his wrists together. Pain and fatigue gnawed at the muscles in his arms and shoulders, vying for attention with the agony of his wrecked eye.

He moaned, but the rag stuffed in his mouth muffled the sound almost completely. The gag tasted like blood and grease, and the texture on his teeth made him want to puke. He tried to spit it out, but it wouldn't budge. Duct tape held it in place and pulled at his cheeks with each facial movement.

Jimmy tried to focus with his one working eye. Everything was fuzzy and a dim. Uneven illumination cast wild shadows across concrete walls and floors streaked with rusty orange stains. Tiny creatures—small mice or giant bugs—skittered beneath the wire shelving lining the walls. They ran across stacked six-packs and in and out of brown boxes with snack-food logos printed on them.

Worse than what Jimmy could see was what he couldn't. A cold, stinking breeze came and went behind him. It tickled his flesh from behind, like some foul demon breathing on his neck. A deep whistle, hollow and nearly imperceptible, accompanied the putrid wind.

Things pittered and pattered behind him as well—chitinous limbs against cement or the quick, rhythmic pattern of a rodent's footfalls. Images of impossibly long centipedes stretching out of floor drains and armies of red eyes glaring from the darkness filled Jimmy's mind.

He struggled against the zip ties and against the pole digging into his back. Neither gave in the least. Tears flooded his eye. He tried once more to scream for help, but the noise could not reach past his gag.

Jimmy didn't want to die there—not in the basement of some raghead mini-mart. How could this be happening, he wondered. It was just a few beers he'd grabbed, and just a dumb joke he'd made. But this—this was insane. This was some legitimate serial-killer shit right here.

His mom had complained about the Arabs quite a bit, about how they pounced on all the small shops and business after the White folks fled to the suburbs in the '60s. She bitched about their price-gouging, about how rude they were, and how bad they smelled. She'd warned him not to fuck with them, though. She'd told him stories about how they cut off the hands of thieves where they came from, and how they stoned their own women to death. She'd told him that no matter how bad-ass he and his friends thought they were, the Arabs were badder.

Jimmy didn't listen to his mom about much, and now he was regretting that.

The room began to spin as Jimmy cried to himself in the dark basement, that foul, pulsing wind kissing him from behind. He closed his eyes and cold and exhaustion crashed over him like a wave. A small worried voice protested, deep in his mind. Some part of him fretted about concussions and never waking up, but that part was not strong enough to keep unconsciousness at bay.

☙

Jimmy woke up with a violent start, and ancient reflexes forced his bound arms to try and ready themselves for a fight. The suddenness of his movements, and the limitations thereon, brought about a terrible pain in his left shoulder.

Somewhere above him, angry yelling and the thunder of gunfire could be heard. Had his boys come back for him? Was the maniac shopkeeper in a shootout with the pigs?

Jimmy screamed for help. He pushed his lungs to their limits, desperate to be heard through his gag. His cries were barely audible, even to himself.

Desperate, Jimmy slammed the back of his head into the metal pole he was tied to. Dull thuds resounded with each strike. It was unlikely that anyone would hear the vibrations through the wooden floorboards and over the chaos and gunfire, but he prayed they would.

An explosion rocked the world above, followed by a whooshing sound and a pained scream. More yelling came after, but it was the wild howls of feral children. It was the sound of his friends. He waited for them to open up some trap door and toss the dead raghead tumbling down the stairs. He waited for them to come cut him loose so he could get to a hospital and see if he still had an eyeball in that shattered socket.

A door somewhere beyond the periphery of his vision opened. A wave of shifting, amber light flooded into the basement, banishing some of the strange shadows and creating more of its own.

Loud, uneven steps echoed on wooden stairs behind him. They were not the quick, light footfalls of a teenage gangster wearing sneakers. These were the slow, heavy footsteps of a grown man, wearing grown-man shoes.

Jimmy pushed his feet down against the concrete and tried to shimmy his back up the pole. Jagged flakes of rust pierced his shirt and cut into his back as he struggled to stand. Thoughts of tetanus came to mind, and he had no clue if his mother had bothered to keep his shots up to date. It was an absurd concern, of course. There were more immediate concerns, like the smell of smoke wafting down into the basement and the angry man who was probably going to execute him.

Seconds later the shopkeeper limped into view. His Magnum hung loose in his grip and his pants were smoldering. The fabric was partially burned away, revealing angry red burns on the thigh beneath.

The Arab walked by Jimmy without a word. He winced with each step, but he shed no tears and his expression was as cold as Scarface or the Terminator.

The shopkeeper grabbed a plastic first aid kit from one of the shelves, ripped off the cellophane wrapping, and opened it up.

He dropped his pants, calmly applied burn cream to his damaged thigh, and wrapped it in gauze. When he was all done, the man pulled his pants back on and turned to face Jimmy.

His eyes were cold—almost black—and they held no mercy behind them. They were eyes that had seen too much—shit that was unimaginable even by Detroit standards. Jimmy thought again about his mother's warnings about not fucking with the Arabs. He thought about women tied to poles, like the one he was currently tied to, getting bludgeoned to death by rocks from their neighbors. He didn't want to go out that way—bound and beaten to death like some cheating bitch. The thought made him pray for the mercy of the clerk's .44.

Jimmy closed his eyes and waited for a racing bullet to scatter his brains or the chrome barrel of the gun to cave in his skull. The shopkeeper's heavy footsteps drew closer. His approach was torturously slow. It felt like minutes between each shuffling step, but eventually he knew the shopkeeper was upon him. He could hear his labored breathing and felt that invisible electricity that buzzes in your skull when someone approaches you.

No Magnum fire echoed from the concrete walls. No steel broke Jimmy's skull like so much brittle porcelain. Instead, he heard the shopkeeper shuffle on past him.

Jimmy opened his eyes and couldn't see his captor. He heard him, though, huffing and puffing as he struggled with something outside of Jimmy's line of sight. The sound of steel scraping against concrete sang an out-of-tune duet with screeching, rusted hinges.

Behind him, the screeching and scraping sounds stopped, but the crackle of fire in the shop above was now audible. Smoke crept in, carrying with it the stink of melting plastic and burning linoleum.

Jimmy couldn't hear the shopkeeper any longer. He guessed the metallic noise had been some door to another building adjacent to this one. The bastard had taken off and left him to burn. Tears ran down Jimmy's face as he stared at the amber glow on the concrete and looked toward the ancient, wooden beams that supported the store. He'd soon be roasted, or crushed under the weight of the building as its compromised structure caved in. Or maybe his death would merge both horrors into a single nightmare—buried alive and slow-cooked by smoldering debris.

Jimmy tried to scream again. He tried to beg the shopkeeper to save him. The gag in his mouth robbed him of his words.

"Stay still," a voice said to him, with only the slightest trace of an accent.

Cool steel pressed against the back of Jimmy's wrist and under the zip tie. A second later he was free. His aching arms fell to his side and he nearly stumbled to the floor. He yanked the duct tape off of his mouth and pulled out the soiled rag, almost vomiting in the process.

He turned around and found the shopkeeper standing with his gun in one hand and a pocket knife in the other. The man's expression was as cold and dark as his eyes. His clothes were burned and in disarray, and a small gold crucifix hung off-center from his neck.

"Grab two flashlights and some batteries," the shopkeeper demanded, gesturing to a set of shelves lined with emergency supplies.

Jimmy nodded and went about ripping open packages of D batteries. His hands shook as he unscrewed the tops of two cheap plastic flashlights and fed the batteries into them. All the while he kept stealing glances up the stairs and through the trap door of the shop where flames were burning brightly.

"What the fuck happened?" Jimmy asked.

"Your shitbag little gangster friends happened. They came back here with Molotov cocktails."

The shopkeeper folded his pocketknife and clipped it to his belt, but kept his gun pointed at Jimmy. He reached out his free hand for one of the flashlights, which Jimmy handed him, careful not to make any sudden movements.

"You go first," the shopkeeper said, pointing to a hole in the wall, roughly a yard in diameter. A rusted cast iron grate hung open, sagging on its hinges, in front of the black tunnel beyond.

Devil's Tongue

Jimmy walked toward the opening, into the cold, putrid wind that blew intermittently from within.

"Where does it go?"

"Away from the fire. That's all I care about. You can take your chances up there if you want."

Jimmy looked toward the staircase. The flames in the shop were just beginning to crawl down the wooden steps. He turned back to the cold, stinking hole and crawled in on his hands and knees.

Jimmy shined his flashlight into the darkness. The tunnel wasn't some simple crawl space dug into the packed earth. It was a man-made thing, formed from ancient bricks and crumbling mortar. It seemed wildly out of place in the basement of some little Arab store off East Warren.

"What the hell is this?"

"Don't know. It was here when my father bought the place. An old storm sewer perhaps. Maybe a bootlegger's tunnel from the prohibition days."

The shopkeeper followed Jimmy into the tunnel. The beams of their flashlights staggered like spectral drunks with each of their movements. Between the erratic motion of the flashlights and the stench on the tunnel's breeze, both of them felt sick to their stomach.

The brick was colder than the air, so cold, in fact, that it was hard to believe that a fire raged in the building behind them and in a hundred others across the city. Even though it was nearly November, and in spite of the icy breeze and cold bricks, small weeds broke through the mortar. Dark, twisted stems strove in the dark and cold, and gave birth to ragged leaves the color of purple lettuce, or devil's tongue, as Jimmy's mama always called it.

"I thought you were gonna kill me," Jimmy said as he crawled forward.

"I'm not a savage like you people."

"You people? What the fuck is that supposed to mean?" Jimmy asked, forgetting for a moment that the man behind was still carrying a Magnum.

"It means I was just going to beat your ass and dump you on the sidewalk at the end of the night. But you people, you came and set my fucking shop on fire after stealing from me. You people tried to murder me just like you murder each other in the streets."

Jimmy huffed and kept crawling forward. The beam from the cheap flashlight barely penetrated the darkness, and there was no end to the tunnel in sight. The deeper they went the colder the air became and the thicker the weeds creeping between the bricks grew.

After a few minutes of crawling the pair came to a branch in the tunnel. They could go straight or turn left. Strange graffiti—nonsense equations and acronyms—were carved into the lower bricks where the two branches met.

COV

$$0 = \sqrt{\frac{1+2}{8*5}}$$

"There's some shit carved in here. You think it's directions?"

"Probably some old bootlegger code."

"Well, you got the gun, so you're the boss. Tell me where to go."

"Keep going straight," the shopkeeper said, after a few moments of contemplation. "The breeze is coming from that direction, which means there's fresh air that way. The other tunnel could be collapsed for all we know."

"I don't know about fresh," Jimmy said, wrinkling his nose at the smell.

The two continued forward on their hands and knees. The tunnel stretched on for a long time with no change other than a downward slope and increasingly dense patches of the dark purple foliage. The occasional bones of a long-dead rodent accompanied by swarms of angry flies helped break the monotony. After a half-hour of crawling both of their backs ached and they decided to take a short break before going on.

Jimmy rolled over onto his back, then sat up so he could look at the shopkeeper. The man was terrifying in the dark. His broad shoulders and full beard were a stark contrast to Jimmy's own wiry teenage frame and pubescent face. The man's dark eyes and severe features were exaggerated by the illumination of the flashlight, making him appear sinister. Only the gold crucifix hanging from his neck made Jimmy feel the least bit of comfort.

"What's with the cross?" Jimmy asked. "I thought all you Arabs were Muslim."

"Not true," the shopkeeper said, shaking his head. "My family are Chaldean. We're Christians. That's part of the reason my parents brought us to America. It's hard for Christians back home."

"My mama's big into Jesus. I like the stories and all that, but I can't really buy into it. I don't see God curing no crackheads, or putting food on people's tables. Jesus ain't there snuffing out the fires on Devil's Night."

"They say God helps those who help themselves."

"Yeah, and that's what we been doing on the streets. Jesus ain't paying the bills. Ford and Chrysler ain't anymore either, so we hustle dope and take what we want. I guess it'd be more pious to get a job at Burger King or some shit and let my family go hungry, right?"

The shopkeeper frowned and shook his head. He offered no argument.

A high-pitched growling echoed from the darkness beyond where they rested. The sound was broken up by angry snorts, tiny squeaks, and the rushing pitter-patter of tiny paws against brick. Jimmy spun onto his belly and shined the flashlight toward the sound. The shopkeeper followed suit and shined his light in the same direction. With a shaky hand he readied his Magnum.

Red eyes gleamed in the darkness for the slightest moment before the thing breached the darkness. It moved so quickly that neither the man nor the boy could tell what it was—just a spastic mass of fur and teeth. Jimmy screeched and fended it off with the end of his flashlight. It bit into the plastic rim of the lens and tried to wrestle the light away from him.

"Drop the light and cover your ears!" the shopkeeper screamed.

"What?" Jimmy asked, never taking his eyes off the bloodthirsty creature. A moment later Jimmy caught the Magnum in his peripheral vision. He dropped the light and slapped his hands over his ears.

The muzzle flashed and the report was like thunder. A bullet raced past Jimmy and struck the ravenous monster, blasting it to pieces and spraying Jimmy with a fine mist of warm, red blood.

"Jesus Christ!" Jimmy screamed. His whole body trembled as he brought his hands down from his ears and retrieved the flashlight. The handle was wet and sticky, and the light shone crimson through the gore-covered lens.

Jimmy wiped the lens with his sleeve, then directed the beam on the dead thing. While the Magnum had utterly destroyed a good chunk of its body, the head was mostly intact. Dead eyes stared back over a long snout and pink nose. Whiskers twitched, maybe from the cold breeze, or maybe just from dying, misfiring nerves.

"It's just a rat," Jimmy said with a laugh. "That was the most pissed-off rat I've ever seen."

The shopkeeper leaned around Jimmy and shined his own light on the carcass. The man shuddered at the sight of the rodent's eyes, still burning with hatred.

"My father told me that back in Iraq the anger and the hate seeped into everything. He used to say it was something in the soil—something that infected the wisest man down to the lowliest vermin. He came here to escape all that, but I think this city is the same."

"I think you might be right."

Jimmy and the shopkeeper sat in silence for a moment, both looking into the dead, angry eyes of the rat.

"We should keep going before more of these things find us."

Jimmy shined his light on the brick floor of the tunnel and did his best to avoid the offal of the dead rat. The dark weeds jutting up between the bricks seemed to seek out the animal's blood. Twisted stems stretched toward scarlet pools and midnight leaves lapped at the carnage … or the breeze going through the tunnel made it seem so at least.

The tunnel branched off a few more times, the same acronyms and equations carved into the brick each time. Jimmy and the shopkeeper kept going straight, following the cold, pulsing wind that surely led to the outside. Neither wanted to chance a branch that could be caved in or lead to some bricked-over dead end.

The further they ventured, the thicker the weeds grew until they were knotted beds of vegetation climbing the walls like ivy. Thorns protruded from stems, which now seemed more like vines. Jimmy found one of the thorns with his open palm. It hurt far more than a simple cut hurts—it ached and swelled like a bee sting.

"Careful, yo!" he called back. "Thorns and shit here."

It was slow going through the patches of barbed vines. There was no avoiding getting pricked, and both Jimmy and the shopkeeper grunted and cursed as they crawled. With each scrape and laceration, Jimmy grew angrier and more miserable.

His thoughts turned to his swollen eye and how the asshole behind him had pistol-whipped him. He thought about the Magnum behind him and how he'd been taken prisoner over a few lousy beers. He thought about his mother's complaints about the Arabs, how they bought up all the little businesses with foreign oil money, leaving Black folks to hustle on the streets.

The shopkeeper was getting testy as well. He cursed at Jimmy, urging him to crawl faster and reminding him that he had a gun on him. Jimmy considered kicking backward and making a move for the pistol. In his mind, he caved in the Arab's nose and took the gun.

His violent daydream was interrupted by signs of hope materializing at the end of his flashlight beam. A rusted grate sagged on a single hinge. Beyond it was a chamber bathed in a faint, purple light.

Elation overcame Jimmy's anger and resentment for the moment. He shimmed across the thorny vegetation and pulled open the grate, crushing and cutting through some of the vines with its weight. Jimmy crawled through and into the chamber beyond.

The ceiling above him was vaulted and he stood tall, stretching his aching back. Tangles of vines, as thick and black as high-voltage cables, covered the floor, climbed the walls, and trailed down from the high ceiling. They wrapped around copper and cast iron pipes that ran through the room, and they grew into them, piercing the metal. Odd flowers—clustered like lavender but far too rich a purple—glowed with faint bioluminescence that faded as that cold, pulsing wind began once more.

A more brilliant radiance replaced the soft light of the flowers. In the center of the chamber sat a massive pod, grown around the base of a spiral staircase. The thing looked to Jimmy like a man-sized artichoke. Overlapping bracts, the same midnight purple of the vines that grew out from it, gleamed with violet brilliance as they spread apart from one another, exhaling that horrible, frigid wind.

Behind the bracts, in the heart of that terrible fauna, Jimmy could see a man merged with the plant. Thorny vines grew into his onyx skin, or perhaps the vines grew out from him. His eyes were bulbous, even closed as they were, and the lids looked like Venus flytraps that had snapped shut.

The breeze ceased as the bracts closed and the illumination died. Light returned to the flowers around the room in response.

"What in the name of Jesus is that?"

The shopkeeper's voice grated on Jimmy's ears, stirring him from his awe of the terrible plant. His body ached from crawling through the tunnel, and the scrapes and cuts from the thorns throbbed in a slow rhythm to the respiration of the pod. This had to be a trick of the mind, he thought. It was a very convincing one, if that was the case.

"We need to go back," the shopkeeper said in a panic. When he turned to head back to the tunnel he found the vines moving of their own accord. They twisted and wove together, blocking off the tunnel.

The light pulsed between the flowers and the heart of the vegetation again. The wretched exhalation of the pod in the room's center battered both men.

The shopkeeper fired at the vines blocking the tunnel. He gave no warning before his shot this time. The sound was deafening and Jimmy's head throbbed along with his wounds, all in rhythm with the breathing of the plant.

"What the fuck is wrong with you?" Jimmy screamed, barely able to hear himself over the ringing in his ears. "Shooting that thing off in here? And at what, some damn vines?"

The shopkeeper spun around, pointing the Magnum at Jimmy. Blood streaked his skin and clothes. His skin swelled in all the places the thorns at bitten him, and the wounds seeped dark venom. It was his eyes that troubled Jimmy—eyes filled with hate like that mad rat they had come across.

"You're right," the shopkeeper responded, turning his pistol on Jimmy. "You got me into this mess, you thieving shit! You tried to rob me! Your friends tried to kill me! I should be aiming at you!"

There was no cover save for the pod and the spiral staircase. Jimmy dashed for the stairs but tripped in a tangle of vines just as the shopkeeper fired. The bullet went over him and into the leathery bracts of the pod at the center of the chamber. The man inside—the man who was merged with the vines and leaves—opened his eyes, revealing intense green eyes with no pupils. The terrible amalgam of man and plant screeched in pain.

The pod—that impossible heart of the vegetation—now glowed with a fierce brilliance, like a violet fire. The vines where Jimmy fell began to tremble and flail. They struck out, but not at Jimmy.

Vines from all around the room reached for the shopkeeper. They caught his limbs and constricted around him. They lashed out like whips and lacerated his flesh. The thorns shredded his flesh, supping upon his blood and offering their own venomous juices in return.

The shopkeeper dropped his flashlight but held onto his gun. He fired one more time, but the plants had pulled his arm off center and the slug flew harmlessly into the wall. The vines encircled his forearm, constricting and stripping his flesh with their thorns. The Magnum fell from his hand as he screamed in agony.

Jimmy forced himself up, despite his pain. Watching as the vines flayed the shopkeeper, he walked over and grabbed the gun from the floor. Even in the agony of his final moments, the shopkeeper wore that same expression of mad rage on his face. Looking into his eyes, Jimmy could see his own reflection bearing the same look of derision that the dying man possessed.

Jimmy could have shot him the face right then. He could have put the Arab bastard out of his misery. He didn't want to, though. Better for him to suffer, Jimmy thought as his aching wounds dripped blood and seeped venom.

The boy turned toward the monstrous creature at the heart of the room. Its eyes were barely open now and a look of something akin to ecstasy was written across its jet-black features. Wet fibers at the edge of the bullet hole in the plant knit themselves together.

Jimmy gave the pod as wide a berth as he could and made his way up the rusted spiral staircase. He took slow, deliberate steps, careful not to trip on the vines or slip on the leaves that ran through the vented steps until he finally reached an access panel in the center of the vaulted ceiling—the one spot not overgrown with vegetation. Jimmy pushed the iron panel open and stared into the darkness above him. He grasped the ledge and pulled himself up, leaving the shopkeeper screaming in the slow, strobing bioluminescence.

***

Jimmy stumbled out from the garage door of the warehouse above the terrible chamber where he'd left the shopkeeper to die. He should have been happy to be alive—he should have been on his knees, kissing the filthy concrete. But he wasn't. Instead, he was filled with hatred and vitriol. His shredded, swollen skin throbbed with pain, and the pain invoked madness.

A siren squelched as a police cruiser turned the corner. The car stopped and a White cop stepped out, holding his gun and demanding that Jimmy drop the Magnum.

Devil's Tongue

Jimmy didn't think about the cop's Glock aimed at him. He didn't think about his mother or his siblings who needed the money he earned dealing drugs and gangbanging. His only thought was how much he hated this White cop, and how full of shit his whole breed was. They'd made Detroit like this—these racist motherfuckers who turned their back on the city because they couldn't stand sharing it with Black folks.

The cop demanded, once again, that Jimmy drop his gun. The young man did the opposite. He raised it and took aim at the cop. Before he could pull the trigger, he was on the ground, wracked with an incredible pain in his chest, and then by the cold of encroaching oblivion.

Jimmy's blood flowed into the gutter where dark, tiny weeds stretched up through cracks between the curb and the street. They moved toward the crimson river and the purple leaves lapped at his blood as if they were the tongues of devils.

No One Leaves the Butcher Shop

Louie held a metal gas can in each hand and stared at the corpse of a two-story home through the eyeholes in his plastic Woody Woodpecker mask. Cracked vinyl siding revealed rotting wood beneath, and the iron railings framing the three stairs to the front door wobbled around freely. All the windows were boarded up with graffiti-covered plywood. Shabby pentagrams and cartoon cocks, shared space with scrawled lines from rock songs and nursery rhymes.

The two Cadillac brothers, distant relations to Detroit's founder, stood on the crumbling stairs. They fancied themselves proper gangsters and wore cheap suits with a bit of criminal flair. The matching cartoon duck masks they wore somehow made them look all the more sinister.

Jasper, the younger of the brothers, carried two five-gallon gas cans, in addition to the ten gallons that Louie carried. The older brother, Hank, wrestled with a crowbar, trying to open the front door that was locked and nailed shut. The wood creaked and cracked, protesting the forced entry. The frame eventually gave way and the door swung inward. A narrow strip of ambient light poured through the doorway, framing Hank's elongated shadow. Utter blackness oppressed the room beyond that sliver of illumination.

Louie and Jasper followed Hank into the house, gasoline sloshing around in the red metal cans they carried. Louie placed the gas cans down and closed the door behind them. Darkness swallowed everything until Hank turned on a battery-powered camping lantern. Yellow light pushed the darkness to the edges of the room, and the roaches followed suit. Shadows, exaggerated and ominous, stretched out from ruined, moldy furniture and across the exposed subfloor and crumbling plaster walls.

"Well, shit," Hank said, stomping his foot on the rotting subfloor. "No one's gonna miss this place."

"The squatters might," Louie said, kicking an empty airplane bottle to the side. "We should make sure the place is empty before we start."

"Why? So some Listerine-swilling hobo can call the pigs on us?" Jasper asked.

"Fuck that," Hank replied, mirroring his brother's sentiment. "Let 'em burn with the rats and roaches."

Louie swallowed hard and eyed the trash on the floor—bottles, cans, and old waterlogged junk mail. He looked to the stairwell leading to the second floor, then into the darkness beyond the doorway on the other side of the room, wondering if they were about to toast some poor bastard. He swallowed hard at the thought but stayed quiet. It was important that this go smooth. He needed the payday.

"I'll take care of upstairs," Jasper said.

The younger Cadillac brother unscrewed the top from one of the gas cans, letting the vapors permeate the air, and pulled a Mini-Mag flashlight from his belt. He walked up the stairway, shining the flashlight ahead of him and trailing gasoline behind.

Louie didn't like the idea of Jasper going off on his own, unsupervised. The guy was an unreliable tweaker, and Louie could imagine him lighting the whole place up with them in it by accident. Hank was running this job, though, and he made the rules.

"I'll get things going in here," Hank said, dousing a mold-ridden couch with gasoline. "You can start priming the next the room."

Louie did as he was told, grabbing one of the gas cans and shining his own cop-style flashlight—a full-size D-cell job that could double as a club—into the darkness beyond the doorway. The ghost of a kitchen greeted him across the threshold. It smelled awful, not just like rot and mold, but like death and rat shit. Linoleum tile was peeling from the floor and wooden cabinets hung crooked against sagging walls. Watery streaks stained the wallpaper—piss yellow in some spots, rusty brown in others.

Flies swarmed above the faucet. Louie shined his light into the sink, finding a pool of viscera—the gutted insides of some animal, or animals. He choked back the vomit climbing up his throat and let out a disgusted curse.

"You all right in there?" Hank called from the first room, his voice muffled by his Halloween mask.

"Yeah. Someone's definitely been staying here, though. The sink looks like a fucking crime scene."

"All the more reason to get this done quick," Hank said.

The counter and kitchen table were lined with trash and old, broken utensils. Louie knocked stiff newspapers, yellowing cookbooks, and crusty wooden spoons to the floor, building a pile of kindling beneath the kitchen table. He uncapped the gas can and the toxic vapor overpowered the stench of death. He doused the table and chairs, along with the garbage kindling he had piled together.

There were two more doors in the kitchen. One was nailed shut, just like the front door, and seemed to lead behind the house. Louie wasn't sure where the other led. It had a keyed deadbolt and it didn't budge when he jiggled the handle and pushed.

Fuck it, he thought. He didn't need to see whatever gross shit was behind there. He splashed gasoline across the door, then poured some underneath for good measure.

Louie turned to douse the rest of the kitchen when he heard a noise from the behind the locked door— a faint a screech, or a cry. He stood still, trying to keep the sloshing gas can steady, and listened. The sound came again, this time unmistakable. It was a cry for help, and it sounded like a child's voice.

"Hank," Louie shouted, placing down his gas can. "There's someone locked up in here."

"Sucks to be them," Hank shouted, making his way from the other room. "They can stay locked up. We're not getting paid to save squatters."

"Come on, man," Louie implored. "We can't fucking burn someone alive."

Hank stepped into the kitchen, flashlight in one hand, crowbar in the other. He shined his light into Louie's face. Louie squinted, then covered his face with his hands.

"We can, and we will. I'm not letting some scabies-ridden loser run off to the cops. Shit, we're probably doing them a favor if this is the best life has to offer them."

"It sounds like a kid!"

All Louie could think about was his own son, working on a homemade Halloween costume with his grandma right now. That's why he was doing this two-bit thug shit, so he could get some scratch together and get his kid the fuck out of Detroit. He'd do whatever it took—starting fires, breaking legs—but God damn, he had his limits.

He couldn't see Hank's expression under the mask. The elder Cadillac stood still and quiet, keeping his light focused on Louie.

"Get that light the fuck out of my face, Hank."

After a few seconds Hank lowered the flashlight, but he remained still and quiet. If he was trying to intimidate him it was working, but he couldn't just let this go. Anxiety tore at him as he waited for some sort of response. The guy wasn't exactly a loose cannon, but Louie didn't think he'd lose any sleep over cracking him with a crowbar and leaving him to burn up with whoever was in the basement.

Another cry for help came from behind the door, simultaneously echoing through the floor below them. The child's voice cracked this time as he screamed.

"Hank …" Louie let the name trail off.

All was silence for a few seconds, save for the buzzing of flies at the sink and Jasper's footsteps on the floor above them. Finally, Hank let out a muffled sigh and took a step in Louie's direction.

"Fine. Get out of the way."

Hank wedged the flat edge of the crowbar between the door and the frame. It gave much more easily than the front door had and swung open to reveal a decrepit wooden staircase that led to the basement. Wavering amber light gleamed from somewhere beneath them, barely illuminating the steps.

"Oh God, is someone there?" a boy's voice called out. "Please don't leave me."

Louie and Hank turned to each other. They nodded in unison, then Hank took the lead, brandishing his crowbar. The steps turned ninety degrees halfway down, and when Hank turned the corner he gasped and stumbled back.

"What is it?" Louie asked, pushing his mask to the top of his head.

Hank ripped off his mask and turned into the corner. He doubled over and began to retch.

Louie hurried down the steps, pushing past him. What he saw when he turned the corner made his knees go weak. He nearly fell down the remaining stairs. "What the fuck?"

Wavering firelight from a wood-burning stove cast a glow upon meat hooks hanging from pipes and rafters. Some were caked with ancient gore. Severed limbs and human torsos hung from others.

An assortment of saws and cleavers littered a work bench topped with a bloodstained wooden butcher block. Piles of charcoal and firewood sat between the wood-burning stove and drums of pink salt. Pickled hands and feet, all too small to have come from an adult, floated in glass jugs set on high shelves. The reek of vinegar and rotten meat was inescapable.

Louie suddenly wished he'd risked the gun charge and brought a piece with him.

A small voice screamed out from a wooden crate in the far corner. Something was thrashing within the box and crying for help. Louie rushed toward the sound, past the carnage and horrifying butcher-shop paraphernalia. Congealed blood from the hanging meat rubbed against his clothes and skin as he hurried past.

"I'm gonna get you out of here," Louie said, in as even a tone as he could manage.

He turned around to look at Hank, who was still hunched over, wiping the vomit from his mouth. He called out, asking him for the crowbar.

Hank looked at the gruesome scene before him. He'd seen death before; he'd even killed a man once. This was something entirely different, however, and he couldn't bring himself to walk past it. Instead, he slid the crowbar across the floor to Louie.

Louie jammed the crowbar into the space where two pieces of the crate met and pulled. The brittle, dry wood split around the nails. He moved the bar over to the left and pulled again. He repeated this until the face of the box was no longer attached to the top.

"Hurry. She'll be back soon."

Louie grabbed the front of the crate with both hands and forced it down like a drawbridge. A little boy crawled out from the box, filthy and naked. He wasn't emaciated as one might expect and even had a bit of weight on him. A chill went down Louie's spine as the implications of this set in. Thoughts of cramped veal pens and witches with candy houses went through his mind.

"Jesus Christ!" Hank called out from the stairs. "This is some straight-up satanic shit, Louie. We need to get out of here!"

Louie tossed his mask to the ground and took off his sweatshirt. He told the boy to put it on. The child slid the shirt over his head and pushed the long sleeves until they were all bunched up and his hands stuck out. The sweatshirt stretched down to his knees, providing warmth and dignity.

Hank was already running up the stairs and out of the subterranean slaughterhouse, yelling for Louie to hurry up. Louie ignored him and turned to the boy.

"What's your name?"

"Kyle," the boy replied, his voice nearly a whisper.

"We're gonna get out of here, Kyle. No one's gonna hurt you."

Louie picked the boy up with one arm and held him close to his chest, hoisting the crowbar over his shoulder. He told Kyle not to look as they walked past the human offal, but he guessed the child had already seen worse than the detritus of these atrocities. He'd probably seen, or at least heard, others chopped and butchered. Louie wondered if a child could ever come back from such an experience.

As they got to the stairs, carefully avoiding the hanging bits of human wreckage, they were met with a stream of gasoline snaking along the wall and down the staircase. Louie rushed up to the landing where the stairs turned, trying not to step in the gas.

Hank stood in the open doorway, pouring gasoline down the steps.

"What the fuck are you doing?" he screamed. "There's an open flame down here!"

"Then you better get the fuck up here!" Hank replied.

Louie carried the boy upstairs, cursing under his breath. He pushed by Hank, who barely moved to let them pass. He put Kyle down and took a deep breath before scanning the area with his flashlight. Whoever had set up shop in the basement might still be in the house.

"Why are you pouring gas down there?"

"So we can finish the job, get the hell out of here, and get paid."

"Screw the job! We need to find a payphone and call this in to the cops!"

Hank tossed the whole gas can down the steps then pulled out a book of matches. He stepped away from the doorway and struck one of the matches. It burst to life with a hiss in the near darkness, its light dancing with shifting shadows across Hank's face.

"There are the bodies of kids down there, man. Those parents deserve some closure."

Hank glared down through the doorway to the basement, lost in thought. He let the match burn down to his fingertips, then tossed it onto the gasoline-soaked steps. Fire erupted and raced down the stairs.

Louie cursed as Hank walked silently back toward the front of the house. He took Kyle by the hand and shined his flashlight ahead of them. As he got to the threshold of the front room he heard the whoosh of a new fire igniting. He turned back to see that the flames from the basement stairs had spread and ignited the gasoline he'd splashed over the back door.

The rest of the kitchen caught quickly. Wallpaper began to blister and burn. The plywood boarding up the windows ignited and breathed out gray smoke. The whole building would go up in no time, but there was nothing Louie could do about it now.

"What the hell?" Hank's voice called out from the front room.

Louie pulled Kyle along with him, rushing into the front room. The camping lantern had died, or maybe someone had shut it off or smashed it. Either way, Louie needed his flashlight to see beyond the doorway. He stopped just past the threshold. The sight before him sent a wave of vertigo crashing over his mind.

※

Jasper dropped a five-gallon gas can at the top of the steps and scanned around with his flashlight. The second floor was in even worse shape than the first. Holes were punched through the plaster walls and light fixtures hung from exposed wires. The smells of piss and mildew mingled in the air. Jasper was reminded of the house he and Hank had grown up in with the revolving cast of stray cats their mother always took in.

The moist carpet squished with each step as Jasper scoped out the layout. There were three rooms on the second floor. A hollow-core door with a fist-sized hole in it sat crooked in the closest door frame. It put up some weak resistance as Jasper pushed it open, its sagging corner catching on the moldy carpet.

Jasper shined his flashlight into a small bedroom. There was no furniture inside, and no trash on the floor, but a series of mounted shelves lined one wall, each holding photographs and newspaper clippings alongside piles of stray paper.

Jasper stepped inside, examining the pictures under his light. They all featured the same man—a heavy-set dude with an old-fashioned mustache and severe eyes. A few pictures showed him with an equally heavy-set woman. Others showed him older, but with a younger woman and baby.

"Looks like Mikey Mustache here traded up," Jasper mumbled with a laugh.

Jasper scanned the next shelf down and found another picture of the same guy, but this time he wore a butcher's apron and cap while smiling between hanging cuts of beef. The newspaper clippings beside it were yellowing crime stories from the Detroit Free Press and advertisements for meats on sale, all from some butcher shop that he'd never heard of.

"Fucking creepy," Jasper mumbled, piling all the photos and papers together into a neat mound of kindling on the lowest shelf. He turned back to retrieve the gas can from the top of the stairs when he heard a noise from the other room. It sounded like an animal—something snorting and scratching behind one of the closed doors.

Jasper left the gas can behind and approached the room where the noise came from. He placed his ear to the door and listened. It was silent for a few seconds, but then another snort sounded from the room beyond.

He retrieved a switchblade from his sports coat and shoved the door open. It was completely dark inside, but he could hear something shuffling around. He cast his flashlight around the room. It was filled with decrepit furniture—an ancient free-standing mirror with broken glass, bookshelves filled with tattered and waterlogged paperbacks, and a stained mattress with rusted springs piercing through the fabric.

"Here kitty, kitty," Jasper called into the room.

Something snorted in the darkness, then moaned. Jasper scanned back and forth with his light, hoping to find an animal rather than a crackhead. This arson job was supposed to be a quick buck, and he did not want to get into a scuffle with some disease-ridden hobo.

He waved the flashlight toward the sound. Something moved through his beam, too fast for him to tell what it was, but certainly bigger than a cat or dog.

"Hey, pal," Jasper called, shining the light around again. "I don't want to hurt you, all right?"

The light caught something again—fat rolls of naked flesh, pink and pale. This time the thing squealed like a pig, then ran away through a massive hole in the wall between this room and the next.

"Fuck this," Jasper muttered, then rushed for the gas can at the top of the stairs.

He stashed the knife in his coat pocket then took the cap off the gas can and tossed it aside. He doused the walls and the moist carpet. Gasoline splashed back, hitting his clothes and his mask.

The squealing came again from the other room, then Jasper heard something shuffling behind him. He dropped the can, letting the gasoline spill on the floor, and swung around with his flashlight. Something rushed at him, but the narrow beam of his light only caught small glimpses of the thing as it ran. A flat snout and lifeless eyes. A massive, pendulous breast swinging freely. A meaty, calloused fist gripping a meat cleaver.

Jasper yelled at the thing, telling it to back off as he reached for his knife. It hit him hard, catching him just below the ribs and lifting him off the ground. It kept running, smashing them both through the railing. Jasper tumbled down the stairs, entangled with his attacker. The wind rushed out of his diaphragm as his back hit the steps and the immense weight of his enemy crushed his chest.

His flashlight rolled down the stairs, clunking away and leaving him in a pitch-black nightmare. The thing on top of Jasper grabbed him by the hair, undaunted by their fall, and slammed his head against the steps, over and over. He felt the skin split at the base of his skull as the creature screeched and snorted on top of him. The ugly sounds faded as his skull cracked open upon the fourth hit against the wooden step. Seconds later Jasper's world went black.

There, illuminated by the beam of Hank's flashlight, was Jasper's corpse. His limbs were broken, splayed out at impossible angles, and the base of his skull was caved in. The cheap plastic duck mask was broken and askew, revealing half his face.

Hank ran to his brother's body. He fell beside him and listened for breathing that never came and felt for a heartbeat that wasn't there. Tears ran down his face as he cradled his little brother. He repeated the word *no,* rocking back and forth.

"It's too late," Kyle said, tears forming in his eyes as well. "She's here."

"Who's here?" Louie asked. "Who did this?"

An angry squeal and a loud snort echoed through the darkness. "The Pig Lady."

Louie dragged the kid over to where Hank sat holding his dead sibling. He shook the elder Cadillac brother and tried to pull him to his feet, but Hank swatted him away.

"We need to get out of here, man! Like fucking now!"

"Give me that," Hank growled, snatching the crowbar from Louie's grip.

The wavering light from the burning kitchen intruded across the threshold, into the front room, but did little to illuminate it. Footsteps sounded from someplace in the dark. Louie waved his flashlight around looking for whoever was stalking them from the shadows. Everything looked monstrous in the narrow beam. Shadows cast from the corners of couches were demons crawling across the walls. The glimmer of the beam on the filthy windows was the aura of a sinister spirit.

Hank lowered his brother's head down to the floor. He was gentle with him—as gentle as when he'd help put him to sleep as a baby. Hank was covered in Jasper's blood. The gore from his brother's corpse dripped from his hand and down the long surface of the crowbar as he stood. The flashlight in his other hand trembled, casting a palsied beam into the darkness. A screech echoed off the walls, and Hank screamed back, not with words but with a sound of sorrow and black rage.

Louie backed up, continuing to sweep the darkness with the flashlight. The beam fell on a figure, but it moved away too quickly for him to process what he'd seen. A rolling mass of blood-splattered flesh? An enormous, hairless animal?

He turned and ran, pulling Kyle along with him and yelling for Hank to follow. He hoped he was running in the direction of the front door, but he couldn't tell for sure.

"I'll kill you, motherfucker!" Hank screamed. "I'll fucking gut you!"

Louie found his way to a boarded-up window instead of the front door. He'd gotten turned around in the dark. He cursed, then followed the wall to the corner and turned. If he hugged the perimeter, he would eventually find the door.

"She's never going to let us leave," Kyle mumbled, his voice trembling.

The boy tightened his grip on Louie's hand and began sobbing. Louie did not try to console him. He simply followed the wall and waved his flashlight back and forth, hoping he might ward off whoever or whatever had killed Jasper.

Hank began to bellow out another threat, but his voice fell short and cut into a gurgle. Louie saw the quick shine of steel and a brief, strobing glimpse of arterial spray as Hank's flashlight tumbled to the floor, end over end. The crowbar slipped from his grasp and clanged against the ground, where it was lost to the shadows. Silenced and disarmed, the elder Cadillac fell where stood. His Maglite rolled back and forth by his dying form, casting a shifting spotlight over his final moments.

Louie hurried along the wall, coughing from the smoke that was filling the house. Finally, he found the door frame. He fumbled for the handle, but the door wouldn't budge. He shined his light across it and found the lock and frame impossibly intact. Even the nails Hank had pried loose were back in the wood, straight, deep, and true.

His head spun and his knees went weak. Bile crept up his throat and his hands trembled as adrenaline coursed through his veins.

He turned, shining his light back into the house and its beam shook unevenly. This time the thing that killed the Cadillac brothers did not run for the shadows. Bathed in the glow of the flashlight, and highlighted by the fire creeping in from the kitchen, Louie could see her in all her terrible glory. Her broad shoulders rose and fell as her giant, sagging breasts trembled with each labored breath. She panted and snorted behind the pig's head she wore as a mask, her eyes as lifeless as the dead hog. Her skin and cleaver gleamed with the fresh blood of the Brothers Cadillac. Old, caked-on gore clung to the hair coming out from under her mask, between her legs, and on her calves.

The fire was crawling across the blistering linoleum of the kitchen, toward the exposed subfloor of the front room. Dark smoke painted with orange highlights warned of the approaching heat, threatening the gallons of gasoline in the room where they stood. In minutes the whole house would be up in flames.

"It's over!" Louie shouted, pushing Kyle behind him. "Your sicko butcher shop is burning down! Just let us go!"

The pig woman let out a snort that might have been a laugh and sauntered toward them, swinging her cleaver in a soft back and forth motion.

"Piggy Peggy bathes in blood slop," Kyle sang the words like a jump-rope song, tears running down his cheeks. "Steals little kids from the bus stop."

It was an old rhyme, going back at least to when Louie was a kid. It was something he'd never given much thought to before—Piggy Peggy, The Hobo Pig Lady. She was a Michigan bogeyman, like the Nain Rouge. She was just a scary story for kids—nothing more.

The pig-faced woman threw her head back and let out a horrid squeal, like a hog being slaughtered, then charged at Louie and Kyle with the cleaver. Despite her size, she moved with incredible speed. She was like a charging boar. Louie shoved Kyle aside, then let himself fall to the ground. The Pig Lady's cleaver bit deep into the wooden door and stuck there.

Louie crawled between her legs as she struggled to free her blade from the door. His hand brushed up against the hair of her legs—it did not feel human. It was too coarse, and it was sticky with the blood of God knows how many victims.

"Takes them to her basement—chop," Kyle was concealed somewhere in the shadows of the room, still singing his haunting tune in between sobs.

Louie's flashlight beam found the crowbar. It was just a few feet away. He belly-crawled as fast as he could, desperate for the weapon. Before he could reach it, and before he was out from under the Pig Lady, she brought her huge, repugnant foot down on his ankle. Something popped. Incredible pain fired across his nerves and synapses. She stomped again. Louie let out a terrible scream as his ankle broke.

"No one leaves the butcher shop."

Above him, Louie heard the sound of the cleaver being freed from the door. He rolled over onto his back and shined his light up at the monster above him. Her weapon free, she turned around and looked down at him. Her heavy, sagging breasts jiggled as she let out another snorting laugh, then fell upon him. The force of her weight suddenly upon him stole his breath. She raised her cleaver above her head and brought it down toward his face, but Louie struck her hand with his Maglite.

The cleaver jumped from her grip, barely missing Louie's face as it clanged against the subfloor. He swung the flashlight at her, knocking her mask askew, and then again at the side of her head. On his third strike, she caught the flashlight, wrestled it from his hand, and tossed it away.

The fire was getting closer all the while. He could feel the heat and smell the gasoline they were lying in. Something had to be done quickly or he was going to die, one way or another.

He fumbled for the cleaver, even as the Pig Lady wrapped her meaty hands around his throat. As her thumbs pressed against his trachea, his fingers gripped the knife's handle. With one clean swing, Louie cleaved through the pig mask and into the skull of the woman beneath. She fell to her side, screeching and convulsing. Her fat digits pawed at the cleaver handle, trying to dislodge it from her face, but it wouldn't budge.

Free from her crushing weight, Louie crawled over to the crowbar. He picked it up by the rounded end and used it to help himself up. Leaning on it like a cane, he hobbled on toward the door on his broken ankle. He gave a wide berth to the monstrous woman who was flailing on the ground.

"Come on!" he yelled to Kyle.

The boy ran over to him and grabbed hold of Louie's T-shirt. They got back to the door and Louie began prying it open with the crowbar. The doorway moaned as the nails gave way and the wood cracked.

The whooshing sound of flame devouring oxygen sounded behind them and a blast of heat washed over the room. Louie turned to look. The kitchen fire had found the trails of gasoline Hank had splashed around the room, and the place went up in an inferno. The Pig Lady wailed as she thrashed about in the fire, while the bodies of the Cadillac brothers burned without protest.

Louie went back to wrestling with the door and the prybar. He needed to get it open, and fast. He had gasoline all over him from rolling around the floor. If the fire got close enough, he'd go up like kindling.

"She's getting up!" the boy yelled.

Louie turned around and could almost feel the hope drain from his body. The Pig Lady was on her feet, burning like some pagan effigy, the bloody meat cleaver nailing her mask to her face beneath. She wobbled for a moment, then found her footing, seemingly unbothered by flame or blade.

Louie gave up on the crowbar and threw his whole body against the door. It gave, but just the slightest bit. He slammed into it again, and again, tears welling in his eyes as Kyle's song replayed in his mind.

No one leaves the butcher shop....

No One Leaves the Butcher Shop

The Pig Lady put her head down and bull-charged them. She screamed something that might have been a word but could have as easily been an inarticulate expression of raw hate.

Louie didn't try to run or dodge this time. He pulled Kyle close to him and stood his ground. As she came into reach, he swung upward with the crowbar, driving the flat blade through her gruesome mask and into her face. He embraced her momentum and leveraged the bar to pull her toward him. She hit the two of them like a flaming cannonball, and all three crashed through the door, sending a shower of splintered wood into the air.

The brick stairs outside the front door battered Louie's back and head as he tumbled down them, even as the fresh, cool air gave relief to his lungs. He lay there, half on the concrete sidewalk, his legs elevated on the steps, and took several deep breaths before forcing himself up.

Louie looked around for Kyle and The Pig Lady, but he was alone. The hollowed pig's head lay burning on the sidewalk. Beside it lay the crowbar and the gory cleaver.

He clutched the sweatshirt he'd given to Kyle to wear. The shirt was empty and the boy was gone. He shook it and squeezed it as if the kid could somehow be hiding in its folds.

Louie called out the boy's name, knowing there would be no answer. He laid his head down on the concrete and wept, waiting for the police to arrive. Sirens wailed in the distance as black smoke billowed from the open door and the boards in the front windows caught fire. An upside-down cross rendered in red spray paint blistered, along with the last line from a nursery rhyme scrawled across the wood.

No one leaves the butcher shop....

Fire Sermon

Brothers and sisters, we are gathered here tonight to join in solidarity against the encroaching darkness! We come together to take a stand—to reject the crime, the pain, and the sin of this world and its prince! We come together as one, to embrace the light!

Beyond these hallowed walls a city is burning. Greedy, weak-willed men scramble about for Satan's shallow offerings. They fight, steal, and destroy for scraps of cash, for reputation and respect, or for simple carnal pleasure. They light fires, desperate for a warmth that they shall never know because they choose to dwell outside of God's light!

But let's talk about fire for a moment, shall we? Fire is a tool born of the Lord. It's a force of purification, from Michael's flaming sword to the ovens that kill the bacteria in our food. God hath rained it upon His enemies in biblical times, and Mother Church used it to purge wickedness and sin not so long ago. Before the lies of the modern age—before rationalist charlatans tried to erase the miraculous, we knew that a barrier of holy fire lay between the worlds we could see and Heaven itself.

So, if fire is a holy thing, why would God Almighty allow the wicked to misuse it? Why, in all His wisdom, would he allow these savages to use a sacred force to kill and destroy? Why would he let destitute men and women get trapped in burning buildings and

Fire Sermon

allow firefighters to perish, choked by toxic smoke or roasted by heat?

Well, the first thing you must remember, and remember this well, is that God makes no mistakes. And second? In His infinite grace, the Lord gave us free will, just as he gave us fire. And why would he bestow such dangerous gifts? Because they are the keys that open the door between this Hell we call Earth—this imperfect creation of the demiurge, ruled by the Serpent of Eden—and Heaven itself. But these keys, brothers and sisters, they must be used in conjunction.

I spoke of the holy inferno that separates this world, and all the others in the night sky, from the invisible and perfect. It is a pure flame, born of God's incredible love, and no wicked thing can pass through it. Only those armored in faith can hope to walk through the burning gates of the welkin and become one with the infinite.

To wear the armor of faith—now that is a choice. And that is what I mean when I say that the keys to Heaven—fire and free will—must be used in conjunction. That is why the vengeful and godless are burning to death across Detroit tonight, and why their deaths shall lead to oblivion—because they are not armored in faith. They play with holy fire as if it were a toy, or they have the hubris to presume they can extinguish that sacred power without seeking God's grace.

But we, brothers and sisters, we know better! And that … that is why we are gathered—to seek out the grace of God!

Now, I see some of you crying in the pews. I see some of you struggling against your bonds or squirming as Brother Holloway and Sister Sylvia approach you with the baptismal kerosene. But fear not, brothers and sisters, our journey is only beginning! Oh, I have such sights to show you! Our shared faith has brought us to this moment—to this celebration of the light and to the precipice of the sacred inferno!

Let the devils have this night. Let them have this whole damn world, in fact! We, brothers and sisters—our congregation that has been so misunderstood and maligned by the unfaithful and uninitiated—we shall soon be one with eternity! Clad in the armor of faith, we shall embrace the cleansing fire, and step through that burning gauntlet purified and worthy to sit at the table of the Lord!

Through Hell for One Kiss

Charlotte passed through the doorway of apartment 303. Once it had been her home ... their home. In a way, it always would be.

It was dark inside, save for the yellow illumination of sodium streetlights shining in through the windows. Even in the dim lighting, Charlotte marveled at the familiar peculiarities of the architecture—the bay window where Andy would play guitar, the slight downward tilt of the hardwood floor, the ancient cast-iron radiators.

The bones of the place were the same, but everything else had changed. It was like this every year when Charlotte returned, new furniture and decorations, but it always jarred her to see their home filled with the trappings of other people's lives. The antique end table they'd refinished with black lacquer was gone, as was the old rocking chair that sat beside it. All the furniture had been replaced by shoddy K-Mart shit—particleboard stuff that cost twice what you'd pay for a decent equivalent at the thrift store.

Even the grandfather clock was gone. Who gets rid of a piece like that? Sure, it had never worked, no matter how much Andy tinkered with it, but it was beautiful. You could feel the sense of history resonating from it—exuding from the pores of the wood.

The burgundy walls had been painted back to some realtor-friendly shade of cream, and the black trim was back to the white it had been when they moved in. It was all wrong.

Charlotte was reminded of a funeral she had been to. The dead woman's mother had the corpse dolled up in a dress and makeup she never would have worn in life. There was a special kind of morbidity to the act, as if the dead woman's identity had been stripped, along with her life. Apartment 303 gave her that same feeling.

The centerpiece of the room was a television, with a VCR and some kind of videogame system hooked up to it. There was no turntable or tape deck in the living room, not even a radio.

Charlotte frowned at this. When she and Andy had called this place home, there had been a stereo where the TV now stood, and milk crates full of records and cassettes instead of stacks of game cartridges and VHS tapes. Different strokes for different folks, she supposed, though the idea that anyone might spend their leisure time watching sitcoms and listening to advertising jingles confounded her.

A framed photo hung in the exact spot where Andy's Les Paul had once hung. The picture showed two young parents and a little boy whose grin was missing the front teeth. They were dressed up in their Sunday best, and the Christmas-themed backdrop screamed department-store photo shoot.

Charlotte wondered if she and Andy would have fallen into this same kind of domestic malaise if life had given them more time together. Would a child have turned them into a stereotypical family? Would Andy have quit playing music and wound up as a bartender or a handyman? Would they have traded evenings drinking in the bay window, listening to The Clash, for watching the Disney Sunday Movie?

She didn't think so. They would have raised a free spirit—a little weirdo like themselves. There'd be no TV. Just books, music, and ghost stories. That was how she imagined it, at least.

Such pondering was moot. Life hadn't given them more time.

Andy's voice came from down the hall, along with the strum of his guitar. This is what called her back, year after year. His song always played here on Devil's Night, and she had as much power to ignore it as doomed sailors could ignore the singing of sirens.

Charlotte called out into the hall, announcing herself to whoever might be here. No one replied. She didn't expect them to. They never did.

There were two doors in the hallway. One led to what had been her sewing room once upon a time. The other led to her and Andy's bedroom. She didn't want to go into the bedroom if she didn't have to. To see another bed in there—another couple—it was too much. The mere thought felt like an incredible intrusion.

The music came from her former sewing room, which she was grateful for. The door creaked as she opened it. An adolescent boy jumped at the sound. He sat on the floor, in front of a Fisher-Price turntable, surrounded by an eclectic mess of action figures, magazines, and records. The clutter told the story of a child on the verge of adolescence.

Mad Magazine and Motley Crüe.

He-man and Hit Parader.

Wonder Woman and W.A.S.P.

And of course, there was her lover's 45—Andy Schraeder, "Through Hell for One Kiss"—spinning on the toy record player.

No one stayed in 303 for long. It was haunted, so people said. Every year there was someone new, but Andy's record always remained. One year a teenage girl found it in the closet. Another year a lonely widow stumbled across it in a drawer. Whoever lived here, they always found it and they always played it.

The boy didn't see her. No one ever did. He stood up, looking a bit concerned and poked his head out through the door. Satisfied that a breeze had blown the door open, he closed it before the music could wake his parents.

He sat back down on the floor, in front of the record player. Charlotte knelt down beside him, swaying to the melody—a melody that was written for her. She cherished hearing Andy's singing and the sound of his guitar. She treasured the words he sang, and never tired of hearing them.

Charlotte wanted more than just the song. She wanted to see Andy's smile, smell his scent, and feel his breath on her lips. What would she do for one more kiss? The same thing she did every year.

The song came to an end. The record popped and hissed before it stopped. The boy picked up the paper sleeve from the floor. A solemn-faced black-and-white photograph of Andy stared out from the sleeve.

"Play it backward." Charlotte's breath was like a cold, March wind on the boy's neck. He shivered and looked around.

"Play it backward."

The boy didn't hear her—not exactly. No one ever did. But her words crawled into his mind, masquerading as his own thought.

He placed the paper sleeve on the floor and turned back to the record player. Pressing his index finger against the vinyl, he spun the 45 counter-clockwise. It hissed and popped for a few seconds before quiet notes began to chime in reverse.

Charlotte was ripped from the present and heaved against the current of time. Years now past battered her soul, as if she were being dragged upriver through furious rapids. Blurry, high-speed images of apartment 303 played out across her vision. The sun rose and set in blinks of an eye, and tenants lived their lives in a mad scramble, like a rewinding video. Eventually, her inertia slowed and time returned to its normal speed, but still in reverse.

The black void and cold numbness that had followed Charlotte's final living moments exploded into a burst of agony and shame. She lay naked, broken, and used upon her bed while the intruders laughed.

The record stopped and Charlotte was back in the boy's room, sitting on the floor beside him. Tears rolled down his cheeks and his hands trembled on the vinyl.

"Keep going," she whispered, embedding her will into his mind. At one time she would have regretted the necessity of dragging the child along for such a ride. Such concerns hadn't crossed her mind in years, though.

"Does it get better?" The boy asked, not sure if he was speaking to himself, or God, or someone else entirely.

Charlotte didn't answer. She knew things were about to get much worse.

The boy rotated the disc again and the music played backward.

The meanest and most violent of the men was now on top of her. Drool was repelled from her skin and rose up in wet strands into his open mouth. The satanic sound of taunts and insults spoken in reverse rolled from his lips. The pain that lit up her nerves faded bit by bit each time his fist pulled back from her skin. Lacerations knit themselves shut and fractured bones mended beneath her flesh.

He got off of her and played with himself for a moment before pulling up his jeans and zipping his fly. She cried as he rubbed his hands together in anticipation, then walked away backward.

The second man took his turn with her and then the first. These two had nearly the same face and they wore similar thrift store suits. They looked like brothers, which intensified her disgust. The numbness of shock gave way to sorrow and fear. Everything was more intense now. Her shame was amplified and her mind more lucid. Charlotte was mercilessly present for every creeping touch and invading thrust.

When the record stopped again, Charlotte saw that the boy's eyes were closed and that his entire body shook. She didn't know if people felt what she did, if they saw her final moments like a snuff film, or if the emotions resonated within them on a more subliminal level. She didn't care. All that mattered was getting through to the other side.

"Keep spinning the record."

The boy shook his head and Charlotte wondered if he had actually heard her, or if he was saying *no* to himself.

"Keep spinning the record," she said more forcefully. Her words were like ice, chilling the boy's flesh and causing him to wince as they hit his brain like an ice-cream headache. He shuddered, then guided the record counter-clockwise.

Notes of an arpeggio swelled and went silent as if they had been sucked back into the strings of the guitar that played them. A reversed and garbled version of Andy's voice called her back through time.

One of the brothers held a fistful of Charlotte's hair. Her arm was twisted behind her back, almost to the point of breaking. The intruder stepped back through the bedroom door, bringing Charlotte along with him. Tears floated up from the floor to her chin and rolled up along her cheeks.

Her own cries sent shivers through her soul—that panicked, coarse screaming that wavered in pitch and rapidly terminated. The entire ordeal was a study in misery, of course, but Charlotte particularly despised the way this part felt—how her lungs expanded with each scream as if she were breathing in her own expelled anguish.

The two of them spun around and Charlotte could now see Andy on the ground in the living room. He lay in a heap by the stereo, his long, dark hair matted with blood and his face a broken mockery. One of the other intruders—the angry one—stood above him with a baseball bat, while another sat in the bay window, fumbling with Andy's guitar.

Charlotte watched thin spires of blood rise up from her lover and climb the wooden grain of the bat. She inhaled sobs as the bastard pummeled Andy's head. His face began to re-form with each hit. His caved-in cheek popped back into shape after one hit. The bat fell upon his face again, and when the intruder brought it back up Andy's nose was straight and intact. Charlotte screeched inverted pleas with each violent strike until Andy was whole and alive.

The song stopped. Vertigo overcame Charlotte as the flow of time righted itself around her. The room spun and the boy was crab-crawling away from the record player. He wore a haunted expression. Charlotte crawled after him, trying to soothe him with words she knew he couldn't hear.

"It's fine. We're almost done, I promise."

She placed her hand upon his cheek. He shivered at her touch.

"We're so close. I just need you to finish the song."

The boy shook his head and stood up. He opened the door, ready to flee the room and go crying to his parents about some nebulous fear he couldn't fully explain or understand. They had come too far to fail, however. Charlotte screeched and the door slammed shut before the boy could leave. He pulled at the knob, but the door would not open.

"Spin ... the ... record."

Frigid cold radiated from the doorknob. The boy pulled his hand away and stumbled back into the room. He fell to his knees in front of the turntable, crying and shaking. In life, Charlotte would have been guilt-stricken for what she was putting the boy through. She wasn't alive, though.

Charlotte urged him one more time, whispering in his ear to spin the record. He did as she commanded and the song played in reverse, transporting Charlotte back to her final day.

Andy rose like Lazurus. His knee straightened as the bat pulled away from it and the intruders sauntered back toward the front door, inhaling their own hateful taunts. They exited apartment 303 and splintered pieces of pine flew into the air before reintegrating with the door and the frame.

Charlotte's panic faded away. They were alone again in their apartment, surrounded by the things they loved. The stereo and piles of records. The grandfather clock that never told time. Andy's Les Paul, leaning against the bay window.

They danced in the middle of the living room, his hands on her waist, hers resting on his shoulders. "Through Hell for One Kiss," the song he had written for her, played on the stereo. It was as beautiful to her in reverse as it was played forward.

"uoy evol I"

Charlotte touched her lips to his and wished that the moment could last forever.

Breaking Wheel

Darkness crept in on Dash's peripheral vision, narrowing his field of view as panic threatened to overtake him. A fog of gray smoke from the hundreds of fires dotting the city obscured the road ahead of him. Neon signs lent an unearthly glow to the haze and burned technicolor afterimages of blurry radiance into his eyes as he sped by.

He couldn't see his pursuers. In his side mirror, they were nothing more than the hazy will-o'-the-wisps of headlights in the ashen mist. He could hear them, though—a half-dozen outlaw bikers howling for his blood. Once they'd been friends and brothers in arms. They'd shared booze and drugs. They'd shared the road. But that was in the past.

Dash felt unsteady on his bike, and his body shook with adrenaline. The faded double line on the asphalt, barely visible through the smoke, was the only thing that seemed real. He concentrated on those lines as best he could, but the danger pursuing him gnawed at his focus.

Acrid smoke burned his lungs with each shallow gasp. Vertigo threatened his balance. He couldn't slow down or stop, though. He was a dead man if he did.

Dash leaned into the upcoming turn, hardly braking at all. He came close to dumping the bike but managed to stay up and right himself as the road straightened out again. His pursuers were more reckless and they hadn't slowed at all for the turn, diminishing his lead.

The radiance of the headlights from the other motorcycles was no longer an obscure glow in the haze, but rather blades of light cutting through the smoke and darkness. Engines growled, louder and louder as they drew closer. War cries of hardened, angry men filled the air.

Something bumped Dash's back wheel. His bike skittered and threatened to topple. The beam of a headlight glared in his peripheral vision, followed by a man decked out in black leather atop a midnight-colored Triumph. In the darkness and smoke, the man and machine looked to be as one—some post-apocalyptic nightmare version of a centaur.

The Triumph bumped Dash's bike twice, trying to knock him to the asphalt. Before it could try a third time, Dash turned his front wheel and struck back. The Triumph toppled, sending the driver skipping across the road and dispelling the illusion that the man and the motorcycle were merged.

A second biker took advantage of this opportunity. With Dash's Harley still leaning to the left, the bike behind him rammed his back tire. Dash's wheels went out from under him. The bike fell, slamming him into the ground, breaking and fracturing sundry bones. His head rattled inside his helmet. The fallen bike crushed one leg and pinned it between the asphalt and the chassis as ruthless inertia dragged him along the blacktop.

The world became a nonsense collage of pain and smoke, of howling savages and hazy light. Then it grew dark and gentle nothingness swept Dash up in its arms.

∽

Dash's mother and father argued in hushed tones, afraid that their argument might scare him, even though he was too young to grasp the meaning of their words. His mother paced back and forth across the living room. His father sat in his recliner, still dressed in his DPD uniform, drinking a beer and staring at the television. This probably wasn't exactly how it all happened, Dash knew that even in his dream, but it's the way he always imagined it.

Sirens wailed outside. Gunshots boomed in the distance. Somewhere in the city, a mom-and-pop store was being looted and the owners would never recover from the loss. Somewhere in the city, a man was being killed by an angry mob because he had too much money and not enough melanin. Somewhere in the city, the police were beating a young man because of reasons just the opposite.

"I don't feel safe here anymore, Russ. You saw those riots last year! What do you think is going to happen now?"

A solemn newscaster on the television was reporting the assassination of Martin Luther King Jr. He spoke with a cold reverence, worry visible on his furrowed brow.

"The same thing that happened last year. They'll riot. We'll quell the riot."

Dash's mother laughed. There was no mirth in the sound. It was an audible expression of disbelief and exasperation.

"They are going to tear this city apart, Russell! Hell, the city is already torn apart. The Riganos and the Pulleos took off to Franklin. Mike and Sandy Boticelli sold their place and bought a gorgeous house in Northville. Anyone with a brain is leaving!"

Dash's father looked over at his wife and tapped the badge on his chest. His expression was stern, but not cold. If anything, there was a fire in his eyes.

"This badge is a promise to serve and protect this city, Janelle. I'm not going to abandon my post. I'm not going to turn this city over to a bunch of lawless savages just because they throw a tantrum."

"What about serving and protecting your family?" Dash's mother was screaming now. "How the hell are you going to do that if you get killed out there?"

"You're going to scare the baby," Dash's father replied in a quiet but severe tone. His mother huffed and wiped tears from her eyes.

Dash's father turned to him. Half of his face was suddenly missing, revealing ragged meat and splintered bone. Bullet holes riddled his chest.

Breaking Wheel

Crimson tears wept from the various wounds, washing down his uniform.

"Don't you worry, little man," his father said, despite missing a good chunk of his lower jaw. "Nothing bad's going to happen to us."

❦

The pain of his shattered femur stirred Dash awake. Breath was elusive, each shallow gasp a painful struggle. He wondered if he might have broken a rib or two when he fell, in addition to his leg.

It was dark, wherever he was, and cramped. He was contorted into something resembling a fetal position, but with his arms behind his back. He tried to move and couldn't. Something—rope or duct tape—bound his hands and feet together.

Music was playing nearby. He could feel each note of "Detroit Rock City" vibrating through the cramped space. There was another rumble coming through the floor, something more quiet and consistent than the sound of KISS.

A sudden sense of movement came over Dash, and it was only then his head cleared enough to realize he was in the trunk of a car. They were taking him somewhere away from prying eyes or curious ears. He began to sob, wishing that his former brothers had just murdered him in the street. Gruesome vignettes played out in his mind—vivid imaginings of what horrible retribution awaited him. Thieves, ironically, had a very strong dislike of being stolen from, and Dash did not believe they would show him mercy.

The car took a sudden turn and the momentum forced Dash forward. His cheek scraped against threadbare upholstery and his head smashed into the steel frame of the trunk.

Dash tried to stay calm and take deep breaths, but he could only manage shallow, labored gasps. He tried to think of a way out of the car, but his gasping lungs and the blow to his head had loosened his grip on consciousness. There was an allure to passing out—an escape from the pain and fear of his current situation—maybe the last bit of respite he would ever know.

Dash closed his eyes.

In real life, the funeral was a closed-casket affair. Dash knew this, but his dreams and memories always stood in contradiction to that truth. This dream was no different, and Dash's father lay in his open coffin, dressed in his policeman's uniform.

Two lines of faceless men and women—impossibly tall grownups— formed a corridor of sorts to the coffin. Dash walked between them, toward his dead father. Their platitudes and sympathies, spoken in deep, almost unintelligible tones, battered his ears as he walked.

So sorry for your loss ...

God has a plan ...

He's in a better place ...

It was the last one that got under Dash's skin. His father had insisted on staying in this necropolis, even after the race riots in the dying days of the '60s and after every White family who could afford to had hightailed it to the suburbs. Not them, though. Dash's old man kept them hunkered down in the city, even as the gangs claimed more and more turf and as life became increasingly violent. He would not abandon his post, even when people started setting the whole damn city on fire every October.

He's in a better place ...

Dash made it through the gauntlet of mourners and stepped up to his father's coffin. The side of his face presented in profile to the gathered was stoic and intact. Standing above his father's corpse, Dash could see the ruined half. Broken teeth heralded a partially missing jaw just past them. Ragged, discolored skin hung over a caved in cheekbone and closed eyelids sagged into a misshapen socket.

He's in a better place ...

Dash cursed his father for keeping them here. He cursed his father for putting them in danger, for surrounding them with poverty and with broken, evil people. He cursed him for putting himself in danger to protect the rabid savages of Detroit, Michigan, and leaving him with no father to guide and protect him.

He's in a better place ...

Most of all, he cursed his father for getting out of Detroit and leaving him and his mother behind.

~

"Wake up, Dash."

The voice that spoke was rough and ragged, born of a half-million unfiltered cigarettes, though its tone was calm and quiet. It was the voice of a monster, at ease in its own lair.

Dash opened his eyes to see a haggard, familiar face above him. Cold and sunken gray eyes stared at him from a face etched with heavy creases and scars. White stubble framed a tobacco-stained goatee and foul, ashy breath wafted past chapped lips and yellow teeth.

"There we go," the old biker said. "Open them eyes."

Dash was lying across two shipping pallets, his arms and legs splayed out and lashed to the rough wood. Splinters and rusted nail heads bit into his exposed flesh. For the briefest moment he struggled against his bonds, but the agony that pulsed through his broken leg when he moved squashed the instinct to try and wriggle free.

"I'm sorry, Frenchie," Dash muttered, tears already forming in his eyes.

"Shhh." The old biker stroked Dash's hair. "None of that, now. You done what you done."

Dash choked back a sob and scanned the room. Tool cabinets and workbenches littered with greasy rags and carburetor parts lined the cinderblock walls. Half-dismantled cars were parked in a neat line, their hoods removed and their insides exposed like vivisection subjects.

He knew the place. It was the garage at Frenchie's salvage yard, a five-acre maze of Detroit steel surrounded by blocks of boarded-up homes and businesses. Rats and squatters were the only souls within the better part of a mile, aside from the bikers who had gathered to watch him die. There was no one to help him here.

A half-dozen bikers had gathered around where Dash lay tied to the pallets. Some wore stoic expressions with disappointment in their eyes. Others gnashed their teeth behind hyena grins. A few looked positively bored and indifferent.

Frenchie sat back on his haunches and retrieved an envelope from the inside pocket of his vest. It was stuffed to the point of bursting, overflowing with cash. Frenchie whistled one drawn-out note as he ran his thumb across the wad of hundreds.

"A for ambition, Dash," the older biker said. "You gotta have close to six figures here. I reckon if you're gonna gamble your life it might as well be worth it, right?"

"It's all there," Dash promised. "I didn't spend a dollar of it, Frenchie!"

"You didn't rightly have the chance, now did you? I'm sure you weren't even gonna stop to gas up until you was well beyond Eight Mile Road. Probably wouldn't have even bought a Big Mac until you was out of Michigan. You didn't make it too far, though, did you, Dash? Don't feel too bad. Motown has a kind of gravity that's tough to escape."

Another biker, a house of a dude named Silver (short for Silverback, due to his enormous size and the ape-hanger handlebars on his Harley), was grunting and struggling with something in the corner as Frenchie talked. It was a massive spoked wheel, five feet in diameter—a crude, rusty thing, made from welded flat stock and rebar.

Silver rolled it across the floor, toward where Dash lay bound. Dash could not imagine what the wheel was for, but it terrified him nonetheless. Hairs on the back of his neck rose up at the grinding sound of it rolling over the concrete. His mouth went dry as the spokes turned, moving ever closer to him.

"That right there is called a breaking wheel," Frenchie said, as Silver rolled massive thing forward and struggled to keep it balanced. "It's a medieval relic used to make an example of thieves, highwaymen, and, of course, of traitors. You check all them boxes, don't you?"

Breaking Wheel

The deep, steady din of the iron rolling across the concrete invoked a knot in Dash's guts. It transfixed him. The turning spokes, not quite evenly spaced and meeting imperfectly near the center, were hypnotic in the most terrible way. Their movement cut past all reason and prodded animalistic fear in the deepest recesses of the mind.

"A wildly inventive bit of cruelty. It reminds me quite a bit of our fair city, in both form and function. Both were born for altruistic purposes—to move man along to where he needs to be. But both got like … corrupted, that's the word. Both got corrupted along the way and became tools with which to crush a man's body and spirit. Hell, the streets of Detroit are even laid out like the spokes of a wheel! I shit you not!"

Dash struggled and squirmed. He bashed the back of his skull against the wooden slat beneath his head. His protests were in vain. The bonds did not loosen and he ended up worse for the struggle, ropes and wood lacerating his skin where he thrashed.

"You wanna know how it works? No? That's okay, 'cause I'm gonna teach you all about it."

"Come on, Frenchie!" Dash pleaded, after he ceased squirming. "You've known me since I was a kid! Damn it, man, you have your money back!"

"I do, and as such, I have no need to barter you a quick death."

Frenchie patted Dash on the cheek and stepped away. Silver pushed the breaking wheel onto the pallet. The brittle wood crunched and broke under the wheel, as did Dash's left shin. The wheel obliterated the bone beneath his skin, leaving the lower half of his leg to match the thigh he'd broken when he'd dumped his bike. The mass of the wheel broke the pallet beneath him, driving splinters deep into his muscle tissue.

Silver held the torture device steady for a moment as he motioned for help balancing it. With some assistance the big man pushed the wheel forward again, destroying Dash's other calf. Frenchie kept rambling, probably a soliloquy on the nature of the oncoming suffering, but his words were drowned out by Dash's cries.

The intensity of his screams tore at his vocal cords, but they eventually quieted into sobs. When they did, Silver repositioned the wheel and ground the errant biker's thighs to pulp. As shock set in, his cries once again quieted, this time into moans.

༄

Dash was cold ... so cold. It was that deep, February chill that burrows down inside your bones. They had no money for heating oil, so Dash made sure to bring his own blanket in to his mother so she could double up before he left for the day. As he tucked her in, even under the padding of the two comforters and a few sheets, he could feel how thin she'd gotten. She muttered a quiet thank you between coughs. He kissed her on the forehead and made his way out the door.

It was even colder outside, but not by much. There was no snow on the ground, and only a few patches of ruddy ice here and there, but somehow the concrete looked more frigid than any field of snow or sheet of ice he'd ever seen. The hungry ground sucked at his warmth, draining his body heat right through the worn soles of his Pumas.

A SEPTA bus drove past. It was headed in the same direction he was, but he didn't have the money to get on. His glance fell on the commuters packed inside, sheltered from the wind and soaking up the heat inside. He was jealous and found himself resenting every one of them. He hated the kids and teenagers who got their bus fare from Mommy and Daddy. He hated the adults on their way to jobs that paid more than a few bucks under the table.

His arms ached from the cold, far more than they should have, and his legs were in agony from the long, early morning walk. Hunger rumbled in his stomach, urging him to eat. He'd given the last of the oatmeal to his mother earlier that morning. She was so sick ... always so sick since Dad passed on. There was no way to justify eating the last of their food himself, even if he needed the fuel to bring home a few dollars today.

They'd meant to leave the city after Dash's father was murdered, but they just didn't have the money, especially since his mother couldn't hold a job with her poor health. They'd get out one day though. For now, they were getting by.

Dash turned the corner to see his high school—his former high school—across the street. He hadn't been sad about quitting. He had never been a good student and making a few bucks sweeping floors at Frenchie's garage beat the hell out of getting his ass kicked several times a week. Still, a twinge of jealousy surged through him as he watched the teenagers huddled around the double doors, joking around and waiting to exploit the promise of warmth and free lunch inside.

He tried to curb his resentment as the bell rang and the doors opened, revealing light and warmth beyond. He tried to remember that each of those kids had their own problems. He made up backstories for them as he watched them enter the building. The kid with the Afro and the Run DMC *patch on his backpack—his dad was doing a dime for running guns. The girl with the pink glasses and the puffy jacket patched up with duct tape was living with her grandparents because her mom was turning tricks. Hell, even the teacher who opened up the doors was mourning his brother who overdosed last week. This city didn't let anyone off the hook.*

All these other slobs were probably going to die here, within blocks of where they were raised. Dash was different. He was going to make some money and find a way out. Maybe the bikers down at the garage would take a liking to him and let him run some errands or deal some weed for them. His dad would have beaten his ass for entertaining such a thought, but his dad was gone, swallowed by the city he'd sworn to protect and serve. Dash wasn't going to make the same mistake.

◦○◦

Agony, unlike anything he had ever felt or imagined, washed over Dash as he woke up. The pain was omnipresent, radiating out from his crippled arms and legs and into the core of his body.

Dash tried to move, but his arms and legs were ruined—torn, pulpy tubes of flesh, filled with splintered bones, ground-up muscle, and ruptured blood vessels. Each limb was threaded between the spokes of the breaking wheel, bending in grotesque angles that no body part should.

A sense of vertigo overwhelmed him. The world spun, on a horizontal axis. The soil of the salvage yard, rich with corroded metal and the offal of dead cars, traded places with the starless, smoke-choked sky, again and again. Dash's head lolled, softly bouncing against the iron spokes of the wheel. Finally, the world stopped spinning and it occurred to Dash that he had been rolled out on the wheel.

He could still hear Frenchie's voice barking orders. Silver held the wheel in place while another biker fastened a chain around the top center spoke. They hooked the chain up to a winch and heaved the breaking wheel into the air.

The gathered bikers cheered. They flicked burning cigarettes at him and pelted him with rusty detritus. Silver grabbed the bottom of the wheel and spun it on its chain. The spinning was too much on top of all the other agony and Dash threw up, spraying the bikers with vomit. A few of them laughed, but most did not. Instead, they threw more rocks and car parts at him, along with a flurry of insults.

It didn't matter that he was ten feet off the ground. The teetering stacks of cars blocked him from view of the road. A car crusher growled in the yard, and far-off sirens screamed into the night, muting the sound of Dash's suffering, not that there was anyone around to hear him anyway. No one was going to come and save him.

Dash closed his eyes and prayed for death.

෴

The hazard lights on Dash's bike blinked in the night. It was late and he was alone on the Ambassador Bridge, save for one or two trucks passing by in the night.

First Dash opened his father's urn. His old man's ashes had been cooped up in there for a long time, so he placed the open urn on the ground to breath as he opened up his mother's. He mumbled a short, improvised prayer for both his parents and poured their urns over the bridge and into the Detroit River.

The falling ashes swirled together, creating a single, descending cloud. For a few moments, the ashes took the form of his parents, dancing on the air the way they would dance in the kitchen during those rare times when his father wasn't working and his parents weren't fighting. He wondered if his mother had missed dancing with his father as much as he'd missed watching them dance. He wondered if she had the luxury to mourn the loss of such things between her bouts of illness.

His mother never had a proper funeral, not the way his father had. She wasn't a cop. She wasn't even a cop's wife anymore. She was just a poor widow, chewed up and forgotten by the Motor City.

Dash imagined that if he had put together a proper send-off for her, some asshole would have told him she was in a better place. But she wasn't. She was still here in this city, swallowed by it like her husband before her. It was like the urban legend about that pig lady … what did the kids in school used to say? No one leaves the butcher shop? Something like that, Dash thought.

She might not be in a better place, but she was better off, at least. No more pain and no more painkillers. No more struggle. Just the cold nothing of her soul dissolved into oblivion, like her ashes dissolving in the river.

As the water consumed the last earthly remains of his parents, Dash felt a weight lift from his chest. He didn't need to worry about his mother finding out about the things he did to support them—the people he'd hurt, the poison he sold to addicts and kids—and he no longer cared about the judgment of his father's wraith. That was all in the past, anchored in this city and in the river below the bridge. He was free now. There was nothing else holding him here.

"Oh, but isn't there?" A voice called out from deep in his mind and echoed off of the water below.

"You have no money and no diploma. You have no skills except breaking legs and running dope. Where will you go? Who will take you?"

Dash wasn't sure who the voice belonged to. Some aspect of his own mind? The city itself? Maybe they were one and the same, intertwined for eternity.

He looked out at the decaying skyline, then down toward the ashes, now lost in the nighttime river. It didn't matter if he was an unskilled lowlife. It didn't matter if he had no money. The city, for all its ugliness, had taught him how to survive. It had taught him how to fight and steal, and he knew just who he could steal from.

Dash dropped the empty urns off the side of the bridge and got back on his bike. He revved the engine, letting the growl of the motor echo in the night, then made his way to empty the safe at the Highwaymen's clubhouse.

⁓

Cold rain and pounding thunder robbed Dash of the mercy that came with unconsciousness. Even though the storm had woken him, he wasn't aware of it yet. Every nerve in his body was screeching, and nothing existed but incredible agony. The pain did not subside, but the rest of reality did come slowly came into focus.

Dash was alone in the salvage yard, aside from whatever vermin were nested among the wreckage and whatever ghosts walked this maze of junk cars. Frenchie and his goons had grown bored with his suffering and gone off to raise hell or pass out elsewhere. Just like that, they moved on with their lives, and he was left as a living corpse strung up among garbage.

His body burned with fever, no doubt from ruptured organs spilling toxins into his blood. The cold rain was his sole relief—the last ally he would ever have in this world. The rest of existence—everything but the rain—loomed around him with plans of avarice. The wind battered the breaking wheel, swinging it back and forth on its chain, straining his limbs and flipping his stomach. Birds and rats watched from the hollows of derelict cars, waiting for the storm to break so that they might pick the flesh from his bones and sup upon the soft nutrients of his eyes.

Breaking Wheel

He tried to call out—to beg Frenchie to come back and put a bullet in him. His throat was too dry and his voice was a mere croak, inaudible below the thunderstorm. Dash leaned his head back into one of the iron spokes and stuck out his tongue, letting the rain run into his mouth and soothe his throat.

As he drank, he began to wonder if the rain really was his friend, or if it was just another chain, binding him to the city and keeping him from his final chance at escape—his last chance to go to a better place. If the rain was another chain, it was a thin and brittle one. Death would come for him soon, though he suspected it would not come as soon as he would like.

Would death even set him free? he wondered. There were a thousand ghost stories in the motor city. Haunted opera houses and haunted apartments. Specters in trailer parks and dead girls in the river. Would he be one more damned spirit, tied to this soil forever, or would he go to a better place?

Dash feared that he knew the answer. Just as his arms and legs were woven into the spokes of the iron breaking wheel, his essence was woven into the spoked streets of the Motor City. The Bible said something about all things returning to whence they came. Ashes to ashes and dust to dust. Mud to mud and shit to shit.

The frigid rain kept Dash awake and fully in tune with his suffering. The thunder pulsed in his head with each strike. He had never been, in his entire life, so consciously and unmercifully aware of his body.

Eventually, the storm calmed, just before sunrise on the morning of Halloween. As Devil's Night came to a close, Dash shut his eyes for the last time, drenched and broken upon the iron wheel. The realization came to him in the last moments of his life that he was not alone on the breaking wheel. In Southwest Detroit a young man was waking up to find out that his father died putting out a fire last night. A girl from Forest Park was making the decision to quit school so she could take care of her little brothers. A mother in Gold Coast was learning that her son pulled a gun on the police and would never make it home again.

They were all one and the same. Drops of blood in shared soil. Rusted spokes on the same wheel.

A Night of Art and Excess

Amelia parked her car, a dying '77 LeBaron, three blocks from away the Oswald. Even from her parking space, she could see the luxury apartment building, stretching into the sky. Its glass and steel exterior reflected the electric glow of the nighttime city. A faint haze surrounded the building—smoke that had drifted in from the fires plaguing the less advantaged regions of Detroit.

The car made odd ticks and creaks, even after Amelia had killed the ignition and removed the key. An acrid smell drifted through the vents from the motor. The car's previous owner had not treated it particularly well, and there wasn't much life left in it. With any luck Amelia wouldn't need it to last but a few more days. She'd be set up after tonight, maybe not for life, but well enough that she could make a life.

She retrieved a wallet-size photograph from her purse and examined the handsome face. The man in the photo had sandy hair that was a bit messy, but in an intentional way that made him just a bit sexier than he would have been otherwise. Full lips smiled above a strong jaw, and blue eyes glared fiercely beneath thick eyebrows. Amelia didn't know the man, but his name was written in red marker across the back of the photo.

Dickon Springate.

A Night of Art and Excess

Amelia took a moment to ponder the type of person she thought might own such a name. It sounded to her like a rich man's name—someone from old money. Was he kind or cruel? Was he in love? Was someone in love with him?

She decided, after musing over the name for a few moments, that it was best not to think of such things. It would just make what had to be done all the harder. The only thing that mattered about Dickon Springate was that he was Amelia's ticket out of her crummy studio apartment and off the pole where she danced.

Amelia slipped the small photograph beneath the hem of one of her long dress gloves, on the inner part of her forearm. It might have been more prudent to discard it in case she was picked up by the police. Having this man's name and picture on her person would be incriminating, but there was a lot of money at stake and Amelia wanted proof that she'd targeted the right man. Men with money—men like her mysterious employer—often tried to double-talk their way out of paying up, and she didn't want her shadowy benefactor claiming that she'd hit the wrong target.

The invitation to the rooftop masquerade was secure in her purse, and it was perhaps the most elegant piece of cardboard Amelia had ever seen. The card stock was light alabaster, mottled with darker grains of cellulose, and trimmed with a gilded floral design that curved this way and that. The body of the invitation was penned in the same handwriting as the name on the photograph.

Miss Amelia Silver,

I request the honor of your presence. Please join my assemblage this coming Devil's Night amid the rooftop garden of the Oswald, for a night of art and excess set against the ambiance of the burning city.

Your servant,
Edwin Earl Echo

A night of excess among Detroit's upper crust sounded positively delightful to Amelia, but alas, tonight was about work, rather than pleasure. There would be time for debauchery down the road, and it would be debauchery on her own terms. No more grinding her ass on drug dealers for a twenty-dollar bill or rubbing her tits in the faces of middle-management suits from GM for half as much. When this was all said and done, she would be the one throwing rooftop orgies.

Amelia stepped out of the car. The late October air was cold and she pulled her mink shawl tight around her bare shoulders. The thing was worth more than her car, but it had been a necessity, rather than a luxury. If you wanted to be rich, Amelia believed, you first had to look the part. The clothes make the woman and all that.

In the trunk was an elegant masquerade mask next to an unopened bottle of tequila. Amelia cracked open the tequila and pressed her lips against the bottle. She swished the alcohol around in her mouth for the better part of a minute, then spit it into the street. She suspected her task might be easier if Dickon Springate thought she was already plastered. Smelling like tequila would go a long way to convince him.

The mask stared up at Amelia from the trunk. A delicate silver latticework gave the mask an elegant, almost feline shape. Sheer black floral lace was stretched across the metallic frame. The eyeholes curved up in an exotic arc and the nose arched sharply down, like a short beak. Black satin ribbons hung from either side. The mask, like the shawl, was quite expensive, but one couldn't go to a masquerade party atop the Oswald looking like a pauper. And she quite literally couldn't afford to miss this party.

Amelia placed the mask over her eyes, careful not to mess up her perfectly spiraled bun, and tied the ribbons securely. She closed the trunk and turned to admire herself in the glass storefront of a nearby restaurant. The reflection was muted and imperfect, but she could see well enough. Her black dress clung tightly to her athletic body, barely containing her breasts. Lace fingerless gloves, the same color and design as that of her mask, extended up to her elbows.

A Night of Art and Excess

She was a vision of beauty and aristocracy, set against the backdrop of a beat-up Chrysler and a bankrupt city. She could almost hear the word "impostor" wheezing amongst the other sounds that her dying car still muttered.

Amelia shook the thought from her head. She was not an impostor. Rather, she had not yet attained her destined status. Her childhood of poverty had been a temporary setback, and her elevation to lower-middle-class was just a stepping stone. She was one of the elite: the world just didn't know it yet.

The Oswald was only a few blocks away, but the cold was already evoking goosebumps across her exposed flesh. Or maybe it wasn't the cold. Perhaps it was the idea of what she had to do at the party—the line she would have to cross.

Dickon Springate. Did he have children? Was he a surgeon who saved lives?

A small hiss escaped Amelia's lips as she dismissed her concerns. Soon enough she could afford to have all the moral crises her heart desired. For now, she was still too poor for such luxuries. Better she be a rich woman regretting what she'd done than a poor woman regretting what she had not.

Amelia's conscience quieted as she crossed the street and walked toward the Oswald. She had worked some private parties for wealthy clients in the past, and she had partied at the homes and on the boats of several local rock stars, but there was no place in Detroit that could equal the sophistication of the Oswald.

The glass doors were trimmed with polished brass and framed in marble. The address was carved in stone, along with the name of the building, rather than expressed via some tacky plaque. There was confidence and permanency to this place.

Amelia approached the building. Her heels clicked against the concrete and then were silenced by the oxblood carpet that extended from the door. A doorman stood beneath the building's overhang, his smart uniform the same shade of deep red as the carpet. He tipped his cap and opened the door while smiling at her from beneath a well-groomed mustache. His eyes never drifted south of her face. He was either gay or a man of impeccable class, she decided. Perhaps he was both.

The inside of the Oswald was even more impressive than its exterior. Hallways of polished marble stretched out in two directions from the foyer. Exotic plants that she could not begin to identify grew from exquisite pots beneath the Greco-Roman reliefs that decorated the walls.

A man in a red opera cape and a black tuxedo was waiting at the twin elevators situated into the back wall of the foyer. A pair of oversized star-shaped sunglasses sat on the bridge of his nose, and Amelia was reminded simultaneously of Paul Stanley and Elton John.

Could this be Dickon Springate? His hair was the right color, a sandy kind of blond, but it was hard to get a proper grasp of his features beneath those giant sunglasses. The distance between them didn't help.

Amelia made her way across the foyer. One of the elevators opened. The man in the opera cape stepped inside and pressed a button on a panel that she couldn't see. The elevator began to close. She rushed over and was able to place her hand in between the doors before they closed. The elevator reopened with a pleasant chime.

She made a show of stumbling into the elevator, acting tipsy, even though she was not. She faked tripping and fell against the man. She latched onto his arms, as if she might otherwise fall, and took special care to press her chest against his as she got her footing. Once she was stable, Amelia looked into the man's ridiculous sunglasses and smiled her best strip-club grin.

"Oh my God! I'm sooo sorry," she slurred, the smell of tequila heavy on her warm breath. "I started my own party just a weeeee bit early!"

A nervous cough escaped the man's throat and his posture stiffened. He reminded her of the eighteen-year-old kids who come into the club for the first time—the real easy marks. She reached up and ran her fingertips along his jawline, disarming him further.

"I bet you're cute under those," she said, pushing his sunglasses up to the top of his head.

A Night of Art and Excess

He *was* cute. He was not Dickon Springate, however. It would be easy to mistake the two from across the room, but not up close. Elevator man's eyebrows were too thin and his cheekbones too pronounced.

"See, I knew you were cute." Amelia pulled the star-shaped glasses back to the bridge of his nose and traded her sexy grin for a drunken half-smile.

"You, um ..." he stammered. "You have me at a ... um ... a disadvantage."

Amelia smiled, sincerely this time. Elevator guy was trying to be smooth, even as he stumbled over his words. It was almost adorable. She couldn't afford to have this sap following her around like a puppy dog all night, though. There was work to be done.

"Oh, I would take off my mask, but I have a wicked case of pink eye. I have to go to the bathroom every half hour and rub away the pus or else my eyelids stick together. Trust me, you don't want to see it."

She hoped that would be enough to turn him off. It was a fifty-fifty shot, she figured. In her experience guys were gross, clueless savages and it took more than a little eye pus to send most running.

"Oh ..." he said, then looked around the elevator awkwardly. Amelia had to hold back a laugh.

A few seconds went by and the elevator was somewhere between the sixth and seventh floors. The man brought his gaze back to Amelia and asked her name. She didn't skip a beat before introducing herself as Ambrosia, which was the name she danced under.

He began to introduce himself, but Amelia didn't care what his name was. He wasn't the man who brought her to the Oswald and that was all that mattered. She pressed her finger to his lips and hushed him.

"Now we're even. I've seen your face. You know my name. I don't want to put you back into a position of disadvantage."

The man blushed at her touch, and she immediately realized she had miscalculated. He took her shushing as a sign of interest rather than the opposite. After another moment of silence, he asked if she was going to the rooftop masquerade. It was a stupid question and it annoyed her, but she answered with a sloppy smile.

"What would ever make you think that?" She followed the question with a snorting laugh, hoping for any way she might kill the perceived mood.

The elevator chimed and the doors opened, mercifully ending the elevator ride. The man took a step back and gestured toward the doors, muttering something about ladies first. She thanked him and did her best to fake an ever-so-slight imbalance to her walk.

An oxblood carpet runner, much like the one outside the building, stretched down a marble hallway that terminated at a set of open doors. An elaborate rooftop garden waited beyond. Amelia could see a number of guests milling about on the other side.

She crossed the threshold to the garden and was greeted by a slender middle-aged man. Unlike the other guests, he wore no mask or ostentatious masquerade garb, but rather a slim white suit. He asked for her invitation with a smile. There was nothing aesthetically startling about his lips or teeth, but his smile made her skin crawl. It was the smile that the butcher gives the cow.

Shaking the paranoid thought from her mind, Amelia handed the gilded invitation to the man in the white suit. He looked it over for a moment and his grin widened.

"Ahh, so glad you could make it," he said with a wink.

He took Amelia's hand and kissed it with a slight bow. She was startled by the softness of his skin and the gentle touch of his slender fingers. She had known the touch of many men, and none had been so delicate or intentional.

"Please enjoy the party," he said, handing the invitation back to Amelia. "And if you would be so kind as to toss your invitation into the fire."

He gestured toward a burning sculpture set atop a concrete pad. The sculpture was a replica, in miniature, of the Detroit skyline. A thick substance, a slow-burning gel of some sort, had been painted over each building, and the tiny city was in flames. Amelia approached the morbid work of art and dropped her invitation into the fire, watching it transform into ash.

It was an odd bit of morbid eccentricity, asking the guests to toss their invitations into the flames that were consuming the effigy of Motor City. She didn't give it too much thought, though. Eccentricity seemed to be the word of the day.

Topless waitresses wearing intricate animal masks handed out champagne and hors d'oeuvres to men and women dressed like horny European aristocrats. Oiled bodybuilders in powdered wigs carried serving trays striped with neat lines of cocaine. Large fur pelts lay scarcely hidden behind exotic bushes and clusters of tiny trees, inviting guests to break away from the main party and explore one another's flesh.

Amelia wished she was here for pleasure. Nothing would please her more than to snort a line and drag some masked man, or maybe even one of the classy ladies, into the garden's recesses and have her way with them. But she needed to keep her head about her. If everything went according to plan she would soon be able to indulge such proclivities whenever she liked.

To become a rich woman, however, Amelia would first need to find her meal ticket—one Mr. Dickon Springate. The picture that had accompanied her invitation and the instructions for the job looked much like a professional headshot, and it was all she had to go on. She had no frame of reference beyond this and didn't even know the man's height. Finding her mark in a sea of masked debauchery wouldn't be easy.

For the first time, she began to wonder why the picture of her target was a headshot, of all things. Was Dickon Springate a model, perhaps? He almost had the looks to be, she thought—high cheekbones, sandy hair, and a pronounced jawline. Come to think of it, he was quite handsome, but not quite Hollywood handsome. Still, she wouldn't mind having a go at him up on the roof before she had to … well, do what had to be done. Nothing wrong with sending the poor bastard off with a bang, right?

Amelia grabbed a glass of champagne from a tray held by a topless waitress who passed by. She eyed the woman's erect nipples and felt a twinge of sympathy for her. Amelia was cold even with her fur shawl. The waitstaff must have been freezing. They were surely getting paid enough to deal with it, though. She also imagined they had indulged in a bit of the catered drugs themselves. With a nice enough buzz, the October air wouldn't be much of a concern.

She strolled through the party, nursing her champagne, eyeing the guests as they mingled and flirted. There were a few men with hair of the same approximate color and length as her target, but their faces were obscured by ostentatious masks.

Amelia made her way to the closest guest who might conceivably be Dickon Springate. His back was turned to her, but the hair was right. She used a tray of shrimp as an excuse to edge by him, snatched a snack up, and turned back around to see his face. He wore a plain domino mask over his eyes, a cheap Lone Ranger–looking thing that might have come from a joke shop. He smiled at her with thin lips, as a slight double chin sagged from his weak jaw. Amelia pretended not to notice and moved on.

As she walked away, biting into her shrimp, the man she had met in the elevator approached her again. She smiled at him and went to move on, but he stepped in her path, holding out a glass of champagne.

"A toast?"

Amelia could see it in his eyes, that desperate fixation that afflicts horny young men. It happened all the time at the club. Some dumb kid would come in on his eighteenth birthday and fall in love with the first set of tits he saw. Usually she didn't mind—all the better for emptying their wallets—but she couldn't have this guy following her around like a lost puppy all night.

"A toast to what?" Amelia asked.

"To …" he dropped his sunglasses down to the tip of his nose and scanned the party. His gaze finally drifted past the edge of the roof and settled onto the fires dotting the city below.

"To being up here instead of down there," he said, his expression taking on a solemn tone.

Amelia could appreciate that sentiment. This was where she belonged, above the clouds of Devil's Night smoke and the hustlers, schemers, and chumps breathing it in.

"To being up here!"

They clinked their glasses together and she took a slow swallow, tipping her head back in an exaggerated manner. He didn't drink. Instead, he watched her, not in the lovesick, puppy-dog way she expected, but with an eerie detachment, as if he were studying the curves of her face.

Amelia found herself spooked by the sudden change to her suitor's demeanor and excused herself. She didn't look back to see if he was watching, but she could feel his eyes on her.

She did her best to forget the creepy encounter and focus on the task of locating Dickon Springate. She strolled through the maze of ferns and abstract sculptures that made up the rooftop garden, singling out all the men with dirty blond hair. There weren't many, and it didn't take much time for Amelia to charm her way into seeing enough of each man's face to discount them as Springate.

Perhaps Dickon Springate was late to the party. Perhaps he wasn't coming at all. Perhaps this was all just an elaborate prank.

A joke? Could this be some terrible, cruel-hearted joke from some jealous bitch at the club?

Amelia suddenly felt very stupid and intensely angry. Of course this was a joke, she decided. Mysterious benefactors don't offer strippers a hundred grand to pull a hit at elite rooftop masquerades. It was the stuff of bad pulp novels. Her face went red thinking of how she'd been duped.

Amelia downed the rest of her champagne. If this was some joke she could at least make the most of the night. There was plenty of booze, cocaine, and sex to be had. If she wasn't going to get rich, she might as well have some fun.

She swapped out her empty champagne glass for a full one and made her way toward one of the well-muscled waiters carrying trays of cocaine. Small glass straws sat on the tray in between the neat white lines. The waiter brought the tray to a comfortable height and Amelia snorted a line.

The coke was strong. It was pure, rich-person cocaine, and it hit her brain like a freight train full of dopamine. Her face went numb and her jaw clenched, and despite her suddenly trembling hands Amelia felt invincible.

Placing the glass straw back down on the tray, she grinned at the waiter and thanked him. There was something familiar about his face as if she'd seen him before.

The jawline.

The eyebrows.

The nose.

Amelia pushed back the waiter's powdered wig. Hidden beneath it was a head of thick, sandy hair.

This whole thing—the letter, the hit, and the hundred grand—it wasn't a joke. Dickon Springate was real and he was here right in front of her. She was going to be rich, or well on her way to it.

But a shirtless waiter? It explained why the picture she'd been sent was a headshot. These kinds of sexy serving gigs usually went to struggling models, but who the hell would drop this kind of money to knock off a nobody beefcake?

Maybe he banged some rich guy's wife, she thought. Maybe her mysterious benefactor, this so-called Edwin Earl Echo, was some rich queer, and Springate had scorned his advances. Amelia didn't really care about the reasons. Only the money mattered.

Amelia ran her numb tongue along her top teeth and took the waiter by the hand. She tried to lead him away, but he resisted. His face bore an expression of inner conflict.

"I really can't," he apologized. "I'm supposed to be working."

"Your job is hospitality, is it not? You serve the party guests?"

Springate nodded.

"Then come serve this guest."

Amelia led Springate past a sculpture that looked like a mass of writhing tentacles, and into a scarcely hidden nook set behind a wall of flowering bushes and small trees. Once concealed from the other partygoers, she pressed her chest against his and brought her lips within inches of his mouth.

"What's your name?" she asked. He introduced himself as Sebastian, and he used the same dishonest tone she used on chumps at the strip club. She couldn't blame him for the lie.

"Do you want to fuck me, Sebastian?" She drew out his fake name, letting it linger on her lips.

He nodded and leaned forward to kiss her, but Amelia retreated, just an inch, denying him her lips. She laughed and ran a single fingernail down his side. Springate leaned forward again, and this time she accepted his kiss.

Springate placed his left hand on Amelia's hip and pulled her tight. His lips were soft, but his grip was firm, as was the substantial bulge in his pants. Amelia ran her hand up his naked back. The smooth, muscular contours of his body felt delightful to her fingertips.

Dickon Springate backed away and knelt down. Amelia was confused for a moment but realized he was placing the tray of cocaine on the ground. She supposed someone would be quite angry if all that white gold were scattered to the wind. When Springate went to stand back up Amelia pressed down on his shoulder, digging her nails playfully into his flesh.

"I think you might better serve me on your knees."

Springate nodded and returned to a kneeling position. He lowered his head and brought his lips to the pointed tip of Amelia's leather boot. She smiled as he kissed her foot and she told him to make her boots shine. There was no reason she couldn't have a bit of fun with her prey. Who would deny the cat the pleasure of teasing the mouse?

Amelia watched as Springate licked the shiny leather of her boots. She loved the way his tongue pressed down against his full bottom lip as he worked his way up. He kissed past her ankle and up the side of her calf, looking up at her with hungry blue eyes.

When he reached the top of the boot, right before her knee, he pressed his wet mouth against her exposed skin. She bit her lip and pushed him back. She pointed down at her other foot.

Springate lowered himself again. He worked his mouth up her other boot, taking time and care to reach the top. There was a sense of practiced passion and awe in his eyes as he looked up at her. It was the same look she gave the men she danced for, and as artificial as she knew it was, it brought her pleasure. It was nice to be the one looking down.

This time Springate paused before bringing his lips to the naked flesh above her boot. This pleased her and she nodded her consent. Springate kissed up past the side of her knee, then pushed her dress up above her hips. She had no panties on, and her wet desire clung to her neatly trimmed pubic hair.

Amelia leaned back and rested her bare ass onto the edge of a massive ceramic pot. Springate pushed her legs apart and ran his lips and tongue across her inner thigh. She moaned as his teeth grazed her skin and his fingers explored her sex.

His tongue teased the uppermost flesh of her thigh. He stopped all at once and looked up at her with a teasing smile.

"May I?"

Amelia grabbed the back of his head in both hands and drove his face between her legs. His hot tongue against her clit sent a chord of pleasure through her. The night air, the cocaine, and Springate's skilled mouth combined to make it feel as if she had lightning pumping through her veins.

Springate pushed Amelia's legs over his shoulders, and she leaned back against the tree jutting out from the pot she sat on. He worked his mouth with fierce passion, running his tongue from her clit to her ass and back up again. She moaned and gasped, nearly losing herself to the pleasure of the moment. This wasn't why she was here, though, and she could not sacrifice her opportunity for wealth at the altar of Venus.

As Springate brought her closer to orgasm, Amelia tilted her head back and removed the long metal hairpins that held her bun in place. She shook her head and long, dark curls cascaded down her back.

She was almost there, so close to climax. Her hips rocked up and down as she fucked Springate's tongue. She came hard and her thighs tightened around her prey's head as she screamed obscenities into the night sky.

Springate's face was still between Ameilia's thighs, and she was still trembling from the intensity of her orgasm when she leaned forward and drove the sharp end of one of her hairpins into the side of his neck. Two streams of blood shot out like twin geysers on either side of the hairpin, painting her thigh red. He howled in pain, but the sound was muffled, his face was still buried in Amelia's dripping sex.

Another stream of blood erupted when she stabbed the second hairpin into the other side of his neck. This stream sprayed her left arm and soaked her delicate lace glove with gore.

Dickon Springate stopped screaming. A wet gurgling noise came from his mouth, and he clumsily pawed at his throat as if he might somehow remedy the damage Amelia had done to him. His strength faded within seconds and Springate fell to his back, his final moments a series of wet, labored gasps.

When he stopped moving—when the sound of his dying had ceased—Amelia collapsed to the cold ground and trembled.

There was a dead man in front of her.

She was a murderer.

She was rich.

It was too much to process, and the music and laughter of the party beyond this hidden nook made the situation unbearably surreal.

All she had to do was make it out of the the Oswald and back to her house. How she was supposed to do that covered in blood, she wasn't quite sure. The reality that she might get caught hit her for the first time. She had just murdered someone, and she could very well go to jail instead of collecting the reward that Mr. Edwin Earl Echo had offered her.

Amelia refused to submit to that idea. She'd come too far. She would make this work. She would not get arrested. She would become the wealthy woman she was meant to be.

Amelia fixed her dress and crawled across the ground, past the corpse of Dickon Springate, and over to the tray of cocaine. She leaned over the tray, on her hands and knees, and snorted another line. The drug hit her hard and banished her fears. She felt confident and invincible.

The arterial geysers from her victim's neck wounds were now dribbling crimson streams. Amelia rolled down the sleeve of her glove and retrieved the photo of the man she was being paid to murder. She compared it to the dead man on the ground, eager to make sure she'd gotten the correct man.

The eyes. The lips. The nose. There was no denying that the face of the corpse matched the picture. Still, she found herself needing more proof that this was indeed Dickon Springate. There had been a few other men who looked similar, and she couldn't afford for this to be a mistake.

She rifled through the dead man's pockets and found a wallet. Inside was a Michigan license with the name Dickon Springate on it. Amelia laughed for a moment as relief washed over her body.

There were pictures in the wallet, too—not of family members or girlfriends, but headshots of himself, the type that desperate models and actors carry around just in case. These were not the only pictures in the wallet, however. There, behind all the headshots of Dickon Springate, was a small photograph of a woman with voluminous blond hair and sharp Slavic features. A name—Heather Tobola—was penned across the back of the picture.

Amelia compared the handwriting on the picture that had been sent to her with what was written on the back of Heather Tobola's headshot. Both names had been penned by the same hand, and both were written with the same red ink.

"What the fuck?" Amelia whispered.

She rose to her feet and straightened her dress. Her skin and her clothes were caked in gore, but there was nothing to be done about that right now. There was no way to clean up and she needed to get off this roof. She just hoped that those who weren't distracted by sex and drugs might be too disgusted and afraid to approach her.

A Night of Art and Excess

A few sets of eyes fell upon her as she emerged from the hidden nook in the garden. She ignored them and strode toward the glass doors and the elevators beyond. A chorus of whispers erupted throughout the party, growing louder and fuller with each step she took. She didn't bother too look back and see if they were talking about her. She knew they were.

The sculpture of the Detroit skyline still burned near the entrance to the garden, and the base of it was black with the ashes of all the burned invitations. Amelia thought back to the invitation, which was also signed in the same handwriting as the picture and the instructions she had been given. Dickon Springate must have received a similar letter with instructions much like those she had received. The girl from the picture in his wallet—Heather Tobola—must have been who he was supposed to kill.

None of it made sense. Why hire Dickon Springate to kill some other struggling model or actress or whatever, and then hire Amelia to murder Springate?

It didn't matter, Amelia decided as she approached the glass doors. She was high on cocaine and adrenaline. Everything would make more sense tomorrow. She would sort it out then.

Amelia tugged on the brass handle of the glass door, but it didn't budge. She tugged again, and when it still didn't open she tried the second door. It didn't yield either.

The slender middle-aged man in the white suit, the one who checked the invitations when she entered, stood on the other side of the door. He did not shrink away from her blood-soaked visage. He didn't even give her a funny look. He just smiled at her and swirled a martini in one hand.

"Can you please open the door?" Amelia said with her biggest, fakest smile, painfully aware of how macabre she must look.

"Of course, my dear," the white-clad man replied. "But not until the party's over."

Someone screamed from deep within the garden. For a moment Amelia was afraid that someone had stumbled upon the corpse of Dickon Springate. Upon turning around, she saw a woman come crashing through a row of plants, her golden, beaked Carnivale mask askew on her face. The young man from the elevator, the one with the star-shaped glasses and the red opera cape, came crashing out after her. He grabbed a fistful of the woman's dark curls and pulled her back to him before snapping her neck in the middle of the party.

The nearby guests retreated as her body collapsed. Amelia watched in disbelief as the boy knelt down, lifted his star-shaped sunglasses to the top of his head, and removed the dead woman's mask. The face beneath was pretty and familiar. It looked almost like Amelia's own.

The young man pulled a small photograph from his breast pocket and compared it to the dead woman. He cursed under his breath and shook his head in frustration. Amelia was suddenly very thankful she had not let him look beneath her mask.

She turned back to the doors. The light from the effigy of the city gleamed against them. A ghostly reflection of the rooftop garden played out on the glass and Amelia could see the guests studying one another: each undoubtedly looking for the victim they'd been hired to kill—each realizing someone was there to kill them.

She tugged furiously on the handles, but neither budged. She screamed in fear and rage. On the other side of the doors, the man in the white suit smiled and raised his glass.

The Work of the Devil

On Maya's twelfth birthday she saw the Devil on her way home from school. He sat on the edge of a dumpster in the alley between Little Caesar's and some bank whose name she couldn't remember. He stared back at her, a cigarette hanging from his black lips. At first, she thought he was a kid in a mask, maybe a fourth- or fifth-grader, judging by his height.

But when he turned to look at her, she could see that the monster's face was not made of plastic or rubber. Those ebony lips curled into a smirk, pushing up crimson cheeks. Yellow teeth clenched around the burning cigarette. The bitter October wind rustled the Devil's midnight locks and his long, patchy strands of beard. Gleaming black eyes like polished marbles glared at her with all the warmth of a Michigan winter. When he winked at her, she knew for sure: this was not some kid dressed up a day early for Halloween.

Maya ran from the alley as fast as she could. She sped the whole way home, lungs burning, and didn't slow until she turned the corner onto Hoyt Avenue. She thought she'd feel safe once she could see her house, but she hadn't been expecting the flashing lights and uniformed men. She hadn't been expecting the firetruck and ambulance. She hadn't been expecting the flames engulfing her home.

Her dad would try to hide it from her, but she'd learn that the fire wasn't set by some Devil's Night arsonist. It was the result of

The Work of the Devil

her mom passing out with a lit cigarette. That's what was written in the official report, at least. But Maya knew the truth. The fire had been the work of the Devil.

In the year following her mother's death, Maya learned all she could about devils and demons. She read the Bible from front to back, watched *The Exorcist* and *Rosemary's Baby* on repeat, and scoured through the library for urban legends and local folklore. She came to believe that the Devil she had seen was a monster called the Nain Rouge—a terrible imp that brought tragedy upon anyone who caught a glimpse of it.

When her thirteenth birthday came around, Maya saw the Devil again. This time she was on her way to school, and the Devil sat drinking in the wreckage of a junked Charger outside of a rundown garage. Her mind was flooded with anger and fear at the sight of his scarlet flesh and charcoal hair. The instincts to fight and flee battled against each other, leaving her paralyzed.

The Devil drank Jim Beam, the same whiskey as her father. He tipped the bottle out through the car window and poured a slug onto the ground. The whiskey seeped down through the loose gravel into the packed, dry earth below.

Panic won out over anger. Maya turned tail and ran to her grandmother's house, where she and her father had been living since their own home burned down. Horrible visions possessed her thoughts as she sped down sidewalks and cut through alleys. Broken traffic lights strobed red, like the flashers of an ambulance. Dead leaves in varying shades of orange and yellow shifted in the wind, like flickering flames. Passing cars exhaled gray exhaust, like the smoke from melting siding and burning wood.

When Maya turned the corner of the block she lived on, she almost couldn't believe what she saw—or more accurately, what she was not seeing. There were no emergency vehicles. No rising flames or black smoke. Her grandmother's house was intact.

Maya rushed inside, afraid that she would find her grandmother dead, but she didn't. The old woman was just fine. Maya collapsed into her arms, crying her eyes out, babbling on about the devil that killed her mother.

Maya's grandmother told her that there was no such thing as the Devil and that sometimes bad things happen for no good reason. She let her take the day off and made her a birthday cake—chocolate with buttercream frosting dotted with chocolate chips along the outer edge. They pored over an old photo album, reminiscing about Maya's mother. It helped dull the pain of that terrible day—the anniversary of her birth and of her mother's death.

As the day progressed, Maya's thoughts turned toward her father. She wondered how he was holding up. He was an old-fashioned kind of man, hardworking and quiet about his emotions, but she knew he was hurting. His pain was as clear in his eyes as it was in the empty whiskey bottles on his nightstand.

The encounter she had with the Devil, or the Nain Rouge, or whatever the hell it was, fell to the back of her mind. Maya was focused on doing something nice for her father when he got home, the same way her grandmother had tried to make the day better for her. Together they prepared her father's favorite meal—a medium-rare steak with thick homemade fries.

Her father always got home by 6:30, so Maya had the table set and dinner ready by 6:15. By 7:00 p.m. the food was cold, and Maya's father still wasn't home. Sometime after 9:00, the police came to the house. Maya watched from the other room as the somber-faced officer told her sobbing grandmother about the car accident.

Her grandmother would try to hide it from her, but she'd learn that the crash wasn't some freak accident. Her father had been driving while under the influence. That's what was written in the official report, at least. But Maya knew the truth. The crash had been the work of the Devil.

On Maya's fourteenth birthday, she refused to leave the house and didn't want any cake or presents. She knew the Devil waited for her, feeding pellets of rat poison to the pigeons in the park or smoking dope in girls' bathroom at school. He waited for her somewhere with a vague portent of doom.

The Work of the Devil

Her birthday demon—the Nain Rouge—could bring no harm to her if she couldn't see him. He couldn't cross her path if she stayed put in the house. The thought occurred to Maya that he might slip through the cracks of the window, like some misty vampire, or crawl up from the toilet like the monsters from *Ghoulies,* so she took precautions the night before.

Biblical prayers were scrawled along the woodwork of the doors and windows. Maya had used lemon juice instead of ink so that her grandmother wouldn't notice and think her mad. She'd mixed holy water she had borrowed from a nearby church with the water in the toilet tank, ensuring that no demon might scramble up from the pipes below the floor. The duct tape she had sealed the tub and sink drains with was more conspicuous than the other steps she had taken to protect herself, but if her grandmother noticed she chose not to address it.

Maya didn't leave her room that morning, and she was thankful that her grandmother didn't come knocking. She stayed in bed and read mindless teen gossip magazines and listened to numbing pop music—anything to keep her mind off of her birthday, the Devil, and her dead parents. After reading every issue of *16* and *Teen Beat* a half-dozen times, Maya found herself feeling hungry and stir-crazy, so she chanced a stroll to the living room.

The house was quiet, save for the sound of her grandmother in the shower. The curtains were still drawn, just as she'd left them. Maya had made her grandmother promise to leave all the curtains shut today, but she was a bit surprised she had kept the promise. The woman detested gloominess and was stricken by claustrophobia whenever she couldn't see the outside.

The television was already on when Maya got the living room. That wasn't odd. Her grandmother often left it on just for the noise.

Maya grabbed the remote control from the coffee table and sat down on the couch. An overly dramatic scene played out on the TV set between a square-jawed doctor and a gorgeous, hysterical nurse. Maya didn't care about their argument over the secret nature of their love affair, so she changed the channel.

She flipped past an episode of *SilverHawks* and past a severe-looking nun doling out spiritual advice. She clicked through fields of monochrome static and skipped the wavy sitcoms that floated up the screen in a repeated scroll. After her next click, the credits to a show were just coming to an end and Maya waited to see what would come on next.

The screen remained black after the last of the white text had shifted up beyond the dimensions of the television. The living room could be seen reflected in the convexed glass of the screen. The Devil lay on the couch beside her in the reflection, black strips of electrical tape crossed like X's over its eyes.

Maya yelped as she jumped up from the couch. Her heart thundered in her chest, but when she looked down to where she'd sat there was no red-skinned dwarf stretched across the cushions— no head of coarse ebony hair leaning on the armrest.

She looked back at the television. The Devil was still reflected in the glass. She edged toward the television to look more closely at the screen. She could see water dripping from his hair. The long strands of his beard were plastered to his bare chest. He didn't move. He didn't breathe.

"Grandma ..."

Maya turned away from the TV and ran past the vacant couch. She felt lightheaded as she rushed out of the room. Her socks lost their grip on the hallway's linoleum tile and she crashed to the floor. A curse shot from her lips as she staggered to her feet and continued to the bathroom.

Water seeped out from beneath the door. Tears rolled down Maya's face and a steady trail of "No"s streamed from her mouth as she turned the knob.

The room was not hot or steamy as it normally was after her grandmother's showers, and she didn't see the woman's silhouette through the shower curtain. The floor was soaked and Maya's socks were instantly saturated once she crossed the threshold. She took slow, nervous steps toward the shower, her sodden feet slapping against the wet floor.

The Work of the Devil

Maya held her breath as she thrust the curtain aside. She exhaled a sob and her knees gave out.

Her grandmother lay naked and face down in the overflowing bathtub. Thin scarlet tendrils floated in the water near her head, diluting into a pinkish mass as they got further away.

Maya reached into the shower to flip her grandmother over, unmindful of how cold the spray of the water was upon her. The woman rolled like a log, buoyant and cooperative. A wicked gash marred her forehead and she gazed at the ceiling with a swollen face and dead, open eyes.

Child Services would try to hide it from her, but she'd learn the seizure her grandmother had in the shower wasn't a random occurrence. She had forgotten to take her medication. That's what was written in the official report, at least. But Maya knew the truth. The seizure had been the work of the Devil.

On Maya's fifteenth birthday, there was no one left for the Devil to take. This time he'd be coming for her, and she told Sadie as much. Sadie, the one person in her class who didn't mind being friends with the "crazy girl," didn't believe her, of course. No one believed her.

Chuck and Francine, Maya's foster parents, didn't give her a hard time about taking the day off from school. They didn't bother her about not wanting to celebrate either. But they made sure she knew there was ice cream in the freezer, just in case. Otherwise, they respected her space.

Sadie, on the other hand, had not. She'd harassed Maya for a week, trying to convince her to come out and have some fun. *It's a Friday, it's your birthday, and it's friggin Devil's Night,* she'd said. Maya had not seen any merit in her friend's argument.

Staying home was the right choice. She was sure Chuck and Francine felt more comfortable with her in the house on Devil's Night, and while she didn't feel any strong bond with them, she appreciated and respected her foster parents.

More importantly, staying home allowed her to prepare. There only were two points of entry into her bedroom—the door and a single window. She had scrawled prayers along the insides of the woodwork to each entrance, just as she had done the year before, but this time she wrote in pencil. The prayers might be more potent, she figured, if they were visible, but also she wanted to erase them before her foster parents noticed.

She'd hunkered down in the corner of the bed where she could keep an eye on both the door and the window. She had everything she needed to stay in the room all day and night—a few sandwiches and bag of garlic and onion chips in case she got hungry (and on the off chance garlic would hold back the Nain Rouge the way it did vampires), her weekend homework, and a stack of lighthearted novels from the library. She even had an empty bucket in case, God forbid, she had to use the bathroom.

Maya was, however, not content to trust her fate to penciled passages on the woodwork and to the grace of God. She had taken other precautions. The sash was locked, as was her bedroom door. Her curtains were drawn shut and taped to the window frame so no breeze might blow them aside. Cheerful pop music played on her boombox. She'd once heard a Bill Cosby skit where he claimed music kept monsters at bay, which seemed to make intuitive sense. And then there was the gun.

Guns weren't hard to come by, not in Detroit. She didn't have money to buy one, but she convinced some wannabe gangbanger at school to let her borrow his for the night. She wasn't proud of how she convinced him, but life had taught her that sometimes you need to do what you need to do.

Evening approached. The wail of sirens waned and waxed as firetrucks and cruisers sped past her window on the way from one emergency to another. Her cream-colored curtains took on hints of red and blue each time they passed, and Maya became concerned that the fabric might not be opaque enough. She feared to see the Devil's silhouette through the fabric.

Maya pushed the thought from her mind and tried to focus on the sound of the DeBarge song playing on her boombox. She opened her math book and considered the first problem of her homework, tapping to "The Rhythm of the Night" with her pencil.

Soon she forgot about the Nain Rouge, at least for a little while. He was never too far from her mind, though. A strange click or creak from the house settling would snap her to attention. The sound of strong wind outside evoked images of howling demons. The stink of the burning city made her think of brimstone fields and the creatures who lived there.

Maya found herself wishing she had invited Sadie to come for a sleepover. She had thought she wanted to be alone tonight—that she needed to hide from the Devil on her own—but now she wanted her friend to be there. It was too late to ask her. Sadie was out on the town, drinking by the river and probably making out with some older guy she'd never see again. Maya was all alone.

Suddenly, Maya missed her parents and her grandmother very much. She wanted to go home, but all she had left was this foster home.

The sound of tapping on the window pulled Maya out of her sad reverie. Her heart went into overdrive and her body trembled as adrenaline surged through her veins. She looked to the window, as ready as she would ever be to face her tormentor. If the Devil was outside, however, she could not see his shape through the curtains.

A slow rhythm of three more taps came from the glass. Maya gripped the pistol, a little snubnosed .22, and climbed out of bed. The gun wasn't heavy, but her hand trembled with the weight of its power. If prayers and holy water couldn't keep the Devil at bay, maybe a bullet could.

The song on the boombox faded out as Maya approached the window. In the silence, she could hear the floor creak under her shaky footsteps.

"Go away." Her voice was quiet but firm.

A loud click startled Maya and she almost dropped the pistol. She spun around, looking for the source of the noise. It was just the boombox, she realized. The cassette had come to an end and the springloaded play button had clicked itself off.

Maya took a deep breath. Before she could regain any sense of calm, the tapping at the window began again. Tears welled in her eyes as she walked toward the sound.

Tap.

"Go away."

Tap.

"Please, just leave me alone."

Tap.

With a shaking hand, Maya threw the curtain away from the window. The duct tape tore away from the frame, taking up some of the white paint, and the curtain rod fell from its bracket, nearly hitting her.

The welled-up tears now leaked down her face. Her bottom lip quivered, out of rhythm with her shaky grip. A sob—the sound of sorrow, fear, and rage—the sound of loss—rose up from deep within her chest.

There, right on the other side of the glass, stood the Devil. The shadows of the tree outside her window obscured his features, but Maya could see his carnelian flesh and the sunken shadows that were his eyes. Ambient light glinted off of his yellow, arrowhead teeth. His scraggly black hair fluttered in the wind.

He had killed her parents. He had killed her grandmother. The bastard had stolen everyone, and now he'd come for her. Maya wouldn't let him win, not this time. She wasn't a little girl anymore and she could fight back.

Maya raised the pistol and aimed it at the Devil's face. He raised his clawed hands and stumbled back from the window. His faux panic made her think of Goethe.

I know nothing more mocking than a devil that despairs.

The gun went off with a pop. Maya stared through the window, with its spiderweb cracks radiating out from a hole in the center. The Devil was gone.

Deeper in the house someone was screaming. Chuck and Francine were in a panic over the sound of the gunshot. This only barely registered in Maya's mind, and it didn't concern her.

The Work of the Devil

She needed to know the Devil was gone for good. She needed to know he was dead.

She turned the sash lock and opened the window. The glass cracked further as she lifted the sash, and razorblade slivers fell from the frame. She ignored the biting shards of glass that fell upon her arms and leaned out the window.

Someone was pounding on her bedroom door. She could hear Chuck screaming, asking if she was okay. She could hear Francine begging her to open up. Maya ignored them.

The Devil lay on the ground outside, a thin geyser of blood spraying from his throat. Something was wrong, though. The monster's face was sideways as if his neck had been snapped, and long golden locks spilled out from beneath his coarse black hair. His neck and wrists were pale and smooth, the skin like that of a person rather than a monster.

"No, no, no …"

Maya dropped the gun and clambered out through the window. She fell upon the Devil's bleeding body, only it wasn't the Devil at all. She pulled the mask away—a cheap rubber thing from a party store—and stared into Sadie's face beneath. The light was fading from her friend's eyes, and she gurgled on her own blood.

Maya had thought the Devil had taken everyone from her. It turned out there was still someone left.

The bedroom door smashed open. She heard her foster parents screaming her name, but her mind couldn't process it. All that existed was her dying friend … the only friend she had.

She put pressure on the wound, as if she might somehow undo the damage, and looked around for someone to help. It was Devil's Night. There were ambulances and fire trucks all over the place, everywhere but here. She did see someone, however—a dwarf with crimson flesh and eyes like polished onyx. He smirked at her from the bus stop, where he stood in front of a poster warning children about the dangers of guns.

Maya screamed in inarticulate rage as a bus pulled up, blocking the Devil from her view. Chuck was outside now, yelling for

Francine to call 911. He forced Maya away from her dying friend. She screeched about the Devil and pointed across the street. When the bus pulled away, the Devil was gone.

Chuck and Francine would try and protect her, but the D.A. would charge her with manslaughter. That's what would be written in the official report, at least. But Maya would know the truth. The shooting had been the work of the Devil.

Rashaam the Unholy

Black boys weren't supposed to listen to heavy metal. That's what the other kids at school said. But Rashaam didn't care what he was or wasn't supposed to do. His room was littered with tapes and records from Venom, Bathory, and Sacrifyx.

Black boys weren't supposed to fall for White girls. Kim's parents sure as hell didn't approve, and neither did his mother. But Rashaam didn't care much for the approval of others. He loved who he loved, and no one could stop that.

Black boys weren't supposed to play their records backwards. That was for bored and troubled White kids. But Rashaam knew there were secrets hidden in the vinyl, and he was going to find them.

Black boys weren't supposed to speak the names of demons. They were supposed to sing in church and be good, God-fearing folks. But Rashaam didn't fear anything—not God nor the denizens of Hell.

Black boys weren't supposed to perform blood rituals or commit human sacrifice. He supposed those were off limits to most folks. Rashaam didn't care about limits. The corpses of Kim's parents and his mother were evidence of that.

Black boys weren't supposed to leave the ghetto. They were supposed to wind up in dead-end jobs or simply wind up dead. But Rashaam was a young man of ambition and power. He uttered his wish to the Devil.

Rashaam the Unholy

The Devil wasn't supposed to grant wishes—not without a catch, at least. But Rashaam didn't care much about the fine print. He took Kim's hand and the Devil led them to a new life outside of Detroit.

The Graveyard
of Charles Robert Swede

Charles Robert Swede, Swede to his friends and the Child Thief to the newspapers, grumbled as he walked across the rotting dock behind his warehouse. It was raining and Swede cursed Sonny Eliot, that no-good weatherman, for predicting clear skies. He was wary of slipping and each deliberate step caused the arthritis in his knees to flare up. The burden slung over his shoulder—a dead child wrapped in a black Hefty bag death shroud—didn't help the pain in his knees. The corpse wasn't heavy, maybe sixty pounds or so, and he was a strong man, but all the muscle in the world couldn't help his aching joints.

Truthfully, he was getting too old for this. Murder—even the murder of a child—was a physically and mentally exhausting feat. And then there was the removal of the organs and the process of wrapping the body. The labor of it all was hard on his joints, and he didn't imagine the excitement of it was great for his heart.

Swede would stop again if he could. He'd stopped before, for almost eight years. The compulsion had been gnawing at his soul that entire time—an evil thing in the back of his mind, dead but dreaming. When he finally acted on that terrible compulsion again, it awoke full of vitality. Now it was stronger than it had ever been.

The Graveyard of Charles Robert Swede

If his knees weren't aching, Swede would have knelt at the dock's edge and placed his burden gently into his motorboat. Instead, he dumped it from his shoulder into the bow. It made a strange, compound noise—the slapping of plastic against fiberglass, set against a wet thud.

Swede set the boat free from its mooring and stepped on. The small vessel was unsteady as he settled into the seat at the stern. He enjoyed that sensation—the uneven wobble of the water beneath him.

He straightened the plastic-wrapped corpse and settled it onto the deck of the boat, then rolled a canvas tarp over it. It probably wasn't necessary to cover the body. It was a rainy Devil's Night and he didn't imagine there would be a lot of other folks on the Detroit River. But there was always the off chance he'd pass by a police boat or some nosy fisherman.

Swede groaned as he bent over the stern and lowered the outboard motor. He pumped the primer bulb, then tugged at the rope start until the motor purred with life.

The boat drifted away from the algae-covered pilings, leaving a choppy wake behind. Swede looked out on the night sky. It was choked with storm clouds and ashen smoke that blocked out the heavens. There was no moonlight; there were no familiar constellations. Just a hazy blanket of burning gray.

The water was its own dark void, however, as black as the veiled cosmos above. City lights reflected off its surface—stars bobbing in the rippling darkness. Soon he would send this broken child into that wet underworld, just as he had with the others. It was, Swede thought, a more noble grave than a plot of dirt beneath a tarnished plaque.

Swede steered the boat downriver and took a moment to appreciate the sites. People tended to shit on Detroit, both out-of-towners and locals, but Swede loved it here. From the gleaming high-rises to the grimy trailer parks, Detroit was home.

He especially loved the river. There was one spot he was drawn to—an unremarkable bit of river northwest of Fighting Island.

That's why he brought the kids out there—so he could keep them forever, entombed in his most special place.

A sense of serenity fell over Swede as his boat glided through the water. He leaned back and enjoyed the passing sights. Rats scrambled in and out of crumbling automotive factories and derelict pump houses. Ancient pilings from ruined docks jutted out from the water like monuments from a sunken city. And above it all, the light of a hundred fires reflected off towers of glass and steel.

"You probably never set foot outside the city, did you kid?" Swede asked the corpse. "You didn't miss much. Screw Paris. Fuck London. To hell with New York. Detroit is the most beautiful city on earth. No better place to live. No better place to die."

The Devil's Night smoke grew thicker in the air the further Swede went downriver. It stung his eyes and robbed him of breath. Worse still, it obscured his view of the shore and of the dark grandeur that was his city.

Swede knew the waters well, but he maneuvered the boat with caution. The Detroit River was a massive body of water, riddled with islands. Some were too large to miss—the nearly thousand-acre Belle Isle and the massive steel refinery of Zug Island, for instance. Others were small enough to get lost beneath the surface when the river was at its highest.

On a clear night, it wasn't a problem. Buoys marked the tiny islands. The lights from his boat only penetrated a few feet through the smoky haze, though.

Swede took it slow and even considered turning back. He could store the body in an oil drum for now, then take it out to his graveyard some other night when he could navigate more easily. That posed other risks, of course. Some busybody might see him dumping the body and call the police. Without the distraction of Devil's Night, they would be more likely to respond. He could get caught.

The thought of being arrested—the thought of going to prison—was enough to spur Swede further downriver and deeper into the smoky haze. Prison was unkind to men like him. He was as much a victim of his compulsions as were the children sleeping under the river, but the run-of-the-mill scumbags in the prison yard would never understand that. Those common criminals—thoughtless, petty men spurred to crime by base desires like money and drugs—could never grasp the black hunger of his soul. They'd beat and rape him, then cave in his skull with a weight. And when he was dead, they would stand over his body and gloat with faux righteousness.

No, he would not be caught. The night and the smoke were his allies.

But there was a lot of smoke. Swede couldn't remember it ever being this bad on Devil's Night in years past. The sky had burned that orange-gray for the past few years, of course, and ashen smoke drifted all across the city, but never this much. He supposed it made sense, though. Every year there were more fires.

Swede followed the natural flow of the river and kept a leisurely pace. Now and then the lights of his boat would fall upon something familiar to let him know where he was—a buoy with a distinct missing chunk or a rock jutting up from the water, covered in bird shit and spray-painted expletives.

The journey to his graveyard was taking longer tonight, but that was okay. There was nothing Swede enjoyed more than being on his boat—well, almost nothing.

Swede rolled the canvas tarp off the wrapped-up corpse on the deck. He ran his hand across the smooth plastic that covered it, taking pleasure in the stiffness of the body beneath. His mind replayed the moment of abduction—the look of fear in the child's eyes, the way he screamed, the feeling of power.

Jagged rocks, mottled with the colors of blood and rust, breached the black water to his starboard side like the spines of some terrible sea-monster. Swede didn't recall ever seeing these rocks before. They had always been there, of course, he assured himself. They were simply too inconsequential for him to take conscious note of under regular circumstances. They only stood out now because of the limited visibility.

There was something else strange going on and it took Swede a moment to put his finger on it. The sounds of the city—the wailing of sirens, the screaming rants of the homeless and insane, the constant din of traffic—it was all so faint in the background.

The silence made Swede nervous. He placed his hand on the corpse once again and squeezed it through its plastic death shroud. This brought him comfort and his mind drifted into safer thoughts. His last kill played out in his mind. The sense of power that came with breaking the boy's neck coursed through him anew, and all Swede's anxiety bled away.

Amber light broke through the smoky darkness ahead of him. Small fires burned on the water—blazing suns set against a cold, black cosmos. It wasn't common, but this happened from time to time. Corporations dumped their waste here. Old ships leaked oil and gasoline. Sometimes it caught a spark.

He'd never seen more than one such fire in a single night before. Tonight he weaved his boat between a half dozen of them.

"It is Devil's Night, I suppose," Swede said aloud. "Fire and flame are the words of the day."

Any familiar landmarks were lost to the veil of smoke and the glare of flame. Burning ash danced in the air, and Swede winced as it fell hot upon his exposed flesh. He gritted his teeth and kept the boat going. Judging by how long he'd been out on the water, Swede figured he had to be close to his graveyard. This would all be over soon.

The lights of the boat fell upon something bobbing up and down in the water. No, not something—someone. The flesh was snow-white beneath streaks of filth—bleached by death and exposure.

Swede trembled. He didn't know whose body it was, but it had to be one of his kills. It had somehow broken free of its death shroud and the weights holding it to the riverbed. How many more had done the same? How long before they were discovered?

The corpse floated face down. Swede brought his boat beside it and reached out. The boat rocked as he leaned over the side and his knees ached from the effort. With a shaky hand, Swede grabbed the dead thing's shoulder. It was stiff—too stiff. Too firm and smooth.

The Graveyard of Charles Robert Swede

Swede flipped the floating corpse over and the plastic face of a mannequin stared back at him. He fell back into his boat laughing and cursing.

The child-sized mannequin floated on its back and stared up at the starless sky with empty white eyes. A permanent grin was etched across its face, and Swede couldn't help but think the thing was laughing at his expense.

Swede settled back into his seat and took a deep breath. Before his nerves could calm, the boat jerked and came to a violent stop. A loud crack echoed across the river: a jagged rock had ripped through the lower part of the bow. Water rushed in through the hole.

"Damn it," he muttered, killing the motor.

There was an old, worn life vest beneath the seat. By the time Swede got it over his head the boat had stopped taking on water. It had filled the bottom third of the boat, nearly submerging the wrapped corpse, but the boat did not sink.

Swede looked out into the black river and couldn't figure out why his boat was not sinking. He leaned over the side and reached his hand down into the cold water. An arm's length below the surface he was met with a jagged rock.

"Shit!" Swede muttered.

He grabbed a flashlight and a flare gun from the boat, then stepped out onto the submerged rock he'd beached himself upon. The cold water came up to his knees, further exciting his arthritis. He groaned as he shined his light across the dense smoke and the dark water.

Fearing that he might get lost in the Devil's Night haze, Swede retrieved a spool of fishing line from the boat. He tied one end to a cleat on the bow and held onto the spool. It trailed behind him as he walked—a lifeline to the boat.

Testing the ground with each step, Swede crept forward, trying to figure out where on the river he'd marooned himself. He swept his flashlight back and forth, looking for any buoys or markers, looking for any break in the smoke that might reveal a landmark onshore. As he continued forward he realized he had not crashed into a submerged rock, but rather a small island hidden just beneath the river's surface.

Swede muttered and cursed about the impossibility of such a thing. He didn't know quite where he was, but there should be no rocky island of this size between his dock and his graveyard. Could he have missed his destination in the smoke and the darkness? Could he have gone so far off track?

Stray outcroppings of rust-colored rock breached the surface, then sank back beneath the water in a slow rhythm. Dark, thorny vines clung to the stone, so tight as to look like the varicose veins beneath the hide of some terrible Leviathan.

The water grew shallow as Swede moved deeper inland. Through the mist he could see that the ground rose above the water and there was a spot where he might sit and wait to be rescued, so long as the river didn't rise much further. He could wait a few hours for the Devil's night haze to disperse, then fire his flare gun and wait to be rescued. Of course, he'd have to get rid of his cargo first.

Something tugged at the fishing line and Swede nearly dropped the spool into the water. It tugged again, harder this time. Swede cursed, envisioning his boat drifting away from where it had run aground and sinking to the bottom of the river. He turned back and rushed across the island, slowed by the water, the uneven ground, and the pain in his joints.

The fishing line jerked again, twice in quick succession, then went slack.

"No!" Swede screamed into the darkness. "No, no, no!"

Stumbling through the water and across the rocky ground, Swede followed the fishing line to its end. It floated on the water. Swede picked it up and examined its end. It hadn't been cut and it hadn't snapped. No, the end of the line was black and melted.

He pointed his light into the water, searching for the other end of the line, but it was gone. A stream of expletives poured from Swede's mouth as he stumbled forward. He prayed that he was heading in the right direction. If he veered off, even by a few degrees, he might never find the boat through the oppressive veil of smoke and ash—if the boat was even there still.

Several minutes passed, wherein Swede plodded miserably through the water. His knees ached. His eyes and lungs burned. Violent fits of coughing left his throat in pain. Eventually he did find the boat, still stuck on the rocks.

The child's corpse was gone from the deck. Its black plastic death shroud floated on the water, split down the middle like a discarded cocoon. Swede stared in disbelief. He scanned the water with his flashlight, searching for the body, but it was gone.

Someone was here with him. Someone had stolen the corpse. There was no other explanation.

"Hello?"

His call was answered only by its echo.

With nowhere else to go, Swede turned back inland, seeking out the high ground he'd found. He tried to stay alert, looking out for figures lurking in the smoky haze. The water rippled in his peripheral vision—a threat of creatures beneath the surface. Floating ash took on ghostly forms, then dispersed into dust.

The water receded and Swede found his way back to the higher ground. He stumbled, climbing upon the uneven rocks, falling on his hands and knees. An amber glow burned from deeper within the smoky haze.

A hollow whistling sounded from further inland—a sound like angry wind blowing through a back alley. Swede was struck by the strange silence of this place. The sounds of the city were gone. No sirens—no car horns—no noise from the auto plants or foundries. All he could hear was the empty howl from the mist and the lapping of water on the rocks.

The sound rose in volume, wavered in pitch, and then faded to silence. It did this again and again, like the respiration of some monstrous beast. Swede could swear the ground beneath him rose and fell with the rhythm.

He pressed further into the smoke, trying to stay quiet. He cursed to himself each time his boots sloshed through a puddle or the pain in his knees elicited an involuntary groan.

Another sound resonated in the silent moments between the intermittent gusts of wind. Several voices chanted in unison. Swede couldn't understand their words.

These were the people that stole his kill. But who would be out in the middle of the Detroit River on a night like this? Satanists? Freemasons? It didn't matter. He could take his chances with them or with the frigid river. It was hardly a choice.

Swede cut his flashlight and crept toward the glow. He felt his way ahead and tested the uneven ground with the toe of his shoe. The amber light within the haze intensified. The chanting grew louder, as did the pulsing, hollow whistles.

Swede tightened his grip on his flare gun. If he could hit one of—whoever—with the flare, the others might scatter. That would give him the chance to slip back into the haze and hunt them down one at a time. Even better, maybe he would find their boat and leave them to the mercy of the cold river.

A figure emerged from the smoke—the silhouette of a child, set against the orange glow. Its posture was off and its head hung limply to one side. Swede shuddered and his grip slackened on his flare gun.

That wind howled again, its wavering tone almost deafening this close. The wind pushed back the smoke, revealing a glowing pit. Dead children were scattered around the edge of the pit. Shreds of duct tape and black plastic death shrouds still clung to some of them. Others were little more than bone, their bodies having been picked clean by scavenging beasts. And then there was the child who stood at the precipice, his shabbily mummified body bathed in the unwholesome light that shined up from the hole in the ground.

He knew them all. Tommy LeFleur. Justin Riley. Mikey Parent. They were all here—all his children.

The din faded. Smoke rushed back into the clear space around the pit, veiling the remains of his victims and transforming the undead thing back into a silhouette. Swede questioned if what he had seen was real.

The Graveyard of Charles Robert Swede

The chanting ceased. A single word, spoken in the small voice of his latest victim, echoed through the night.

"More …"

Swede flinched and coughed as the wind picked up again, blowing the smoke into his face. The smoke cleared once more, banished by the gusts that wailed from the pit. The child—the corpse—that stood at the edge locked his cold gaze on Swede. Its eyes were lifeless and unremarkable, just as they had been in those moments following death.

"More …" The voice boomed over the terrible wind, but the child's mouth didn't move.

Swede stepped forward, his eyes darting from the remains of one child to the next. It was impossible, but somehow his underwater graveyard had risen above the surface. That perfect, magical spot beneath the water—that necropolis where he kept his most prized treasures—he was walking on its sacred ground.

"More?" Swede asked.

The wind stopped again, and smoke filled the vacuum. The silhouette of the dead child collapsed, its form lost to the night and the smoke. A new specter rose within the orange haze—a skeletal figure, broken and misshapen. It reminded Swede of a mistreated toy.

"More …" this new monster implored.

Swede edged closer to the pit as it exhaled again. He closed his eyes to the barrage of wind and smoke. He opened them to the sight of a small malformed skeleton, its bones held together by mud and seaweed. Scraps of plastic refuse clung to its ribs.

The skeleton pointed to the dead child who had just collapsed. Its head lay upon a jagged rock and a stream of blood ran across the ground, into the pit.

Swede clambered over the corpse and gazed into the hole. The rough stone walls were riddled with branches of luminous orange, like veins of molten steel pulsing through the rust-colored rock. The skulls and ribs of children clung to the side of the pit—hundreds of charred bones merged into the stone. Skeletal hands clawed at the air and blackened skulls squirmed on sagging vertebrae. Desiccated corpses struggled within shadowed crevices.

Smoke obscured the depths of the pit. Swede couldn't gauge how far down it went, but there were so many dead, more than he could kill in a lifetime. It was the most beautiful thing he could imagine.

Swede wanted to join them. He yearned to throw himself into the smoke and the light—to bathe in the amber glow and stay with the beautiful children for all eternity.

"More ..." a legion of voices cried in unison. Some called from the abysmal depths. Others spoke through Swede's victims whose ruined bodies encircled the edge of the pit.

"One more," Swede muttered heaving himself over the rim.

He crashed into a shallow pool. The otherworldly pit vanished, along with the countless dead—a rippling illusion on the water's surface. He groaned as he sat up, hurt and confused.

The pit was little more than a puddle, and while the bodies of his victims still encircled it, none of them were animated with unnatural life. They laid still and dead, just as he had left them.

The earth shook beneath Swede's feet and the oppressive smoke dissipated. Water rose around him, swallowing the rocky ground—swallowing the bodies of his victims.

Swede now understood why he'd been drawn to this spot. He understood why he couldn't bring himself to lay his children to rest anywhere else. He looked down, desperate to catch one more glimpse of that other world—that infernal graveyard that had called him to this spot for so long. It was gone.

The ground gave out under him as the island sank beneath the river. He fell beneath the surface, then bobbed up, gasping and treading water.

Sirens and car alarms faded in over the eerie silence. Smoky haze evaporated into the night, revealing the electric lights of the Detroit skyline and the glow of a hundred burning buildings. Rotted pilings jutted up around collapsed docks.

It was all so lackluster—all so mundane. The streaks of neon graffiti across concrete facades held little beauty compared to the molten veins running through the living stone of that other world. Shambling crackheads and junkies were counterfeit reminders of the alluring, writhing dead that dwell in that amber light.

Swede shed his life vest and dived beneath the water. He stared into the depths of the river. No light glowed below. No dead children stared up at him. There was only blackness.

"More …" The word echoed in his mind.

"More," Swede agreed.

He would bring more. He would bring as many as it took.

This City Needs Jesus

Archbishop Edmund Gorecki gripped his rosary beads and muttered a prayer at the corner table of the dive bar. It was not the type of place he would go on his own, but the occult investigator, a man named Adze, had insisted on meeting there. The archbishop stared at an untouched glass of red wine on the table. Anxiety had his stomach in knots, and the thought of sipping cheap wine from a dirty glass made him want to vomit.

A boisterous female bartender with long red hair and a skintight Blondie T-shirt was lighting shots on fire at the bar. Molotov Cocktails, she called them—a Devil's Night special. She was alluring, and Gorecki hated that his eyes were drawn to her.

"I wouldn't mess around with her," a soft voice cut through the drunken ruckus. Gorecki jumped, nearly spilling his wine.

A man in a tattered olive drab jacket—presumably the man he had come to meet—had seemingly materialized from the shadows. He spun a chair around and sat down, resting his arms across the back support. "I understand you've been looking for me, priest."

The archbishop found the man unsettling to look at. His skin was a vitiligo patchwork of rich, earthy brown dotted with porcelain spots. Feral copper irises glowed around his dilated pupils. Dreadlocks, bound together in a ponytail, stretched down past his shoulders. His features were sharp and gaunt, like those of a B-movie vampire.

"Adze?" It was a stupid question, of course, and the archbishop regretted asking it right away. Who else could it be that emerged from the shadows with eyes glowing like fireflies? Of course, this was Adze, son of the Devil.

It was doubtful that Adze could back up his claims of infernal lineage, but looking at him in person, the archbishop was certain that there was something unnatural about the man. The exact nature of the man's strangeness didn't matter, however. What the archbishop cared about was the fact that Adze was the most respected occult investigator in Michigan (insofar as such a profession is respected), and that he was known for having little concern for morality or law. An ambiguous sense of ethics would be important for what had to be done.

"I assume you didn't invite me here to share a glass of wine."

Adze spoke in a hushed tone, barely more than a whisper, yet his voice cut through the noise around them, almost muting the chaos. It was as if his words took priority, and all other sound made way when he spoke.

"I'm afraid not," the archbishop said with a frown. "I have a job for you. It's somewhat sensitive in nature. I need it dealt with quickly, efficiently, and with discretion."

Adze picked up the glass of wine from the table and guzzled it down. He licked his lips, exposing a set of gleaming white teeth that were almost movie-star perfect, if a bit too sharp on the canines, then nodded his understanding.

"Quick, quiet, and clean. I can do that," Adze responded. "What's the gig?"

"There's a decommissioned church, Saint Agnes', where an excommunicated priest has been squatting and following unsanctioned religious pursuits. Mother Church would like it if he were to vanish without further incident. The same for anyone else in there with him. It would be best if they were ... unburdened of this earthly toil."

Adze placed the glass on the table and eyed the archbishop. His gaze fell upon the holy man like a weight on his chest.

"You're leaving something out. Why pay someone like me to sweep out a squatter or two? Why not call the cops?"

A sigh escaped the archbishop's lips and he lowered his head before answering. The pressure of the situation, the intensity of Adze's person, the terrible secrets he held—it all threatened to suffocate him.

"The priest, Father LaVelle, is quite mad. The pain and sin overbrimming on the streets of our city—overbrimming throughout the world—have proved too much for him. He seeks answers. No, he seeks a solution—something beyond the parameters of decency and faith. He's performing heretical rites within the abandoned church. The archdiocese would rather the details of those rites stay quiet."

Adze nodded his understanding. "Let's talk about money."

―※―

Gray storm clouds mingled with black smoke in the sky above Rosa Parks Boulevard. It was late, nearly midnight, but the night glowed with the chaotic radiance of the city. The work of a hundred arsonists imbued the hazy sky with an otherworldly glow, highlighted with the occasional strobing of red and blue.

Adze stood across the street from St. Agnes', studying the massive arched windows in the front for any sign of light or life within. There was nothing—not that he could see at least. From where he stood he'd guess that the old church housed no one, save for a stray cat or two and maybe a small army of pigeons. Of course, the archdiocese wouldn't have offered him five figures to clear the place out if it were that easy.

No one leaves alive. Those were his instructions, though not in those words. The archdiocese had spoken in soft-bellied euphemisms, which were somehow more unsettling than plainly stating he wanted everyone in the building dead. It left him wondering what kind of company the archbishop had expected Father LaVelle to be keeping.

This City Needs Jesus

Adze crossed the empty street, examining the façade of the church. Red brickwork made up most of the exterior. White masonry framed the windows and the three doors along the front of the building. Green ivy and dark vines climbed the tower on the left side of the building, leading up to a high steeple topped with a patinated cross.

The building was in good shape and didn't look abandoned, at least if you ignored the *No Trespassing* signs. The archdiocese had only closed the doors to Saint Agnes' a few months back, and entropy had not yet taken its toll. Perhaps that's why Father LaVelle had chosen to set up shop here: the fact that the neighborhood was sparsely populated, at least by city standards, with one out of every four houses boarded up and covered in gang tags.

Adze took special care not to touch the iron railing of the steps to the church. Iron did not agree with him. His mother had always said it was a medical condition passed on by his father. He supposed she was telling the truth, in a way.

The three oak doors, set into stone arches, all looked tight and secure. Adze placed his ear up to the center door, listening for any sound inside. He hoped he would be met with silence, but that wasn't the case. Someone was moaning and crying behind those doors. The sound was soft and it might have been missed by someone with more pedestrian senses, but Adze had a knack for picking up on sounds and smells that others missed.

He unlocked the middle door with the key given to him by the archbishop. As the door swung open, the putrid air hit Adze like a breaking wave. The unmistakable stench of death permeated the chapel within.

Faint ambient light from the night sky filtered in through the giant windows above the front doors, casting a dim path of illumination down between the pews and terminated at the altar. Around the altar lay three small forms, each covered in a purple sheet. The one in the center was aligned straight with the front of the altar. The others were set at 45-degree angles, forming a sort of arrow pointing toward the altar, or perhaps pointing past it to the effigy of Christ on the wall.

Adze sniffed the air for signs of anyone else in the chapel, but the smell of death was overwhelming. He listened intently and scanned the area for any sign of Father LaVelle. His night vision was excellent, and he was sure that no one hid in the shadows. He could still hear quiet sobs from deeper within the church, though, as well as low, repetitive mutterings—a chant perhaps.

Adze's feet made no sound as he approached the altar. He knelt down and removed one of the sheets to find exactly what he feared he might. A little boy lay beneath, lifeless and clad in a simple white robe. His was face bloated and blue. A ring of dark bruises decorated his neck. The boy's right clavicle was visibly broken, along with the matching shoulder.

The other bodies were the same, but in varying states of decay. They were all little boys, not one of them a day over nine years old, each dressed the same and each bearing similar wounds. Adze feared that the sobbing he heard was that of a fourth child about to be added to that body count.

Adze stepped out of the muted light from the windows and into the shadows at the back of the church. He followed the sounds of muttered prayers and fearful sobs past the altar and through a door in the back of the chapel. He closed the door behind him, hoping to cut off the scent of the corpses.

This room was completely dark, and even Adze's superior senses had their limits. He retrieved a well-worn Zippo from his jacket pocket and flicked the wheel. A flame came to life, offering glimpses of the room, which appeared to be a study of sorts. A candle sat on an old rolltop desk, next to stacks of leather-bound tomes and reams of notes. He lit the candle and flipped the lighter closed.

Adze took a cursory glance at the books. To the layman they might have seemed an eclectic mix—old Bibles and gospels purged from canon, tales of Arthurian legend and Celtic paganism, books on Hinduism and ancestor worship. Adze could see a common thread within the books, however—resurrection and reincarnation.

Adze flipped through the notes on the desk. They were written in a rushed, shorthand cursive that was hard to make sense of. Beyond the messy handwriting, there was a controlled chaos to the note-keeping that Adze couldn't wrap his head around. Lines stretched from one circled phrase to words underlined in the margins. Esoteric symbols floated above the ends of quoted passages like superscripts or exponents.

The terms and phrases he could make out began to paint a picture. Lunatic scrawlings rambled on about *Samhain, the Day of the Dead,* and *the veil between worlds.* Talk of sacrifice littered nearly every page, from quotes about the biblical Crucifixion to examples of the Celtic tradition's threefold death.

Threefold death ...

Adze thought back to the bodies around the altar. Each of them bore a trifecta of deadly wounds: broken bones, as if they'd died from falling; the gallows bruises around their necks; the bloated visage of the drowned with which each corpse stared back at him.

With the candle in one hand, Adze left the study and walked through a door to the left, which brought him to a long hallway that looped around toward the front of the building. The hall was dark, but faint glimmers of light reflected off the ground past the far doorway.

The sounds he had heard before were more pronounced here. The chanting prayer echoed through the hallway from somewhere beyond the far threshold. It was more audible and articulate now—repeated phrases uttered in some dead language. The soft cries, almost certainly those of a young boy, could also be heard more clearly.

Adze crept down the hallway, his eyes scanning the small radius of candlelight with each step. A new smell, a potpourri of stagnant water, mildew, decaying leaves and bird shit, wafted from beyond the threshold. Adze stepped through the doorway to find a shallow pool of filthy water, perhaps six inches deep, filling a divot at the bottom of a stairwell. His candle's light reflected off the murky water and the wet orange leaves floating on the surface. Below the surface he could see Enochian sigils—angelic script—spraypainted in a ring at the outer edges of the pool.

A staircase climbed high up into the steeple, twisting around in an angular spiral. The noontide light of the burning city filtered through windows and open arches, casting strange shadows down the steeple's interior. Adze extinguished his candle and followed the voices that echoed from the landing high above him.

Despite the careful and deliberate nature of Adze's footfalls, the aged wooden steps creaked loudly. He stopped immediately and so did the chanting. The crying persisted, however, and an impatient shushing noise came from the landing at the top of the steeple. Adze flattened himself against the wall, ducking into the shadows.

"Who's there?" a voice called down from the top of the steeple. It was hoarse and frantic.

An old man in purple vestments looked over the railing and down the stairwell. His white hair was unkempt, his skin dark and wrinkled. He held a burning censer in one hand and a pistol in the other.

Adze considered his options. He could rush up the spiraling steps and hope that the priest wasn't a good enough shot to hit a target moving between the crisscrossed shadows of the stairwell. Alternatively, he could use one of the dark gifts that were his birthright. It was clear which was the more prudent option, though he grimaced at the thought.

He closed his eyes and let his body dissolve into the darkness. The pain of doing so was excruciating, and it never got better, no matter how many times he did it. While he had never gotten used to the agony, he had learned to manage it. Far worse than the pain was the time spent in the cold and vacuous waste of the shadow realm. It only took seconds for Adze to travel from one darkened place to another in the real world, but that same time in the black aether felt like hours to him.

When Adze re-formed he was on the platform at the top of the steeple, hidden in the darkest corner. A young boy, clad in ivory robes, stood crying beside the priest. A noose made from rough hemp rope stretched from the child's neck up over the steeple's rafters, and was tied to a cleat on the wall. There was little slack keeping the boy from choking, and he trembled with fear.

Adze stepped out from the shadows, and the little boy gasped. Father LaVelle hushed the boy without looking back and scanned the darkness below. Adze brought his index finger to his lips, imploring the child to stay silent, but the boy was too scared.

"Help me," he sobbed.

This time Father LaVelle turned around. Upon seeing Adze he stumbled back, almost falling heels over ass down the stairs, but the priest managed to find his footing. Madness danced behind the holy man's eyes and the muscles in his face twitched and contorted.

"You … Judas reborn … child of the demiurge … you've come to stop the rebirth."

"Something like that," Adze replied, edging forward.

"It's too late," the priest said with an expression of insane determination. "The veil between worlds is at its thinnest. The stars are right and the same breach that allows devils to drive these streets mad will serve as the means for God to return!"

"You know Detroit as well as I do, padre. The stars don't shine in our sky and all our gods are dead. Killing that little boy won't change any of that."

A look of indignation and disgust crossed Father LaVelle's face. His lips pursed and his eyes narrowed as he put himself between Adze and the child. The priest's body language was almost protective.

"You think this is murder?" He screamed the question. "Murder? This is mercy and sacrifice. I am sending this boy to heaven so that he might give his body as a vessel for Christ!"

"Like those other kids downstairs?"

Father LaVelle's face spasmed and a twitch ran through his entire body. Tears welled in his eyes. His lips pulled back, revealing gnashing teeth.

"It will work this time! It has to work this time!"

"No one else needs to get hurt," Adze lied, raising his hands in a gesture of peace. "Just put the gun down, Father. This city doesn't need any more pain or bloodshed tonight."

"No, this city doesn't need more pain," the priest said, hurling the burning censer at Adze and flinging the boy over the railing. "This city needs Jesus!"

Adze covered his face and the censer crashed into his arms. It opened, raining smoldering incense all across his clothes and his skin. It burned, first the way fire does, then in that chemical, lye-on-wet-skin way that blessed objects sometimes affected him.

He fell back, hissing into the darkness and willing his body to dissolve into the shadows. The priest fired his pistol, but Adze was already gone. A cloud of embers—the burning incense from the censer—floated to the ground where he had been.

The confused priest nudged the shadows with his foot as if the darkness were a material thing. Meanwhile, the child hung from a rope above the hollow of the stairwell. He gasped and flailed, clawing at his noose.

Adze re-formed in the dark corners atop the rafters. He stared down at the confused priest, then over at the swinging child. He cursed the archbishop's directive to leave no survivors.

With a curse on his lips, Adze dove from the rafters onto Father LaVelle. The two of them crumpled into a pile on the floor, and the priest lost his grip on the gun. The pistol skittered across the floor and off the platform, down into the abyss of the stairwell.

LaVelle tried to wrestle Adze off of him, but he couldn't overpower him. Adze was younger, stronger, and he was no ordinary man, though even he himself wasn't quite sure what the truth of his own pedigree was.

Adze punched Father LaVelle in the face, knocking his head against the floor. With the priest dazed, Adze scrambled to his knees and tried to pin LaVelle down by his shoulders. The old priest was more resilient than he'd expected. He swung his right arm up, clobbering Adze's neck with a set of rosary beads wrapped around his forearm. The relic brought upon the same chemical-burn pain that the incense had, and Adze reeled back.

The priest lashed out again, this time smashing the rosary into Adze's mouth. His bottom lip blistered and split open. Adze staggered and reeled back onto his haunches. LaVelle did not squander the opportunity. He squirmed free and drove one foot squarely between Adze's legs, sending him onto his back.

Father LaVelle staggered to his feet, Adze's blood sizzling on his rosary beads. The child had lost consciousness and swung dying and limp. He needed to cut him loose before it was too late to enact the second phase of the threefold death.

The priest produced a dagger from the folds of his robe, an ancient weapon bearing the seal of the angel Samael on its pommel, and ran to where the noose was anchored to the wall. With a rushed prayer of resurrection on his lips, he brought the blade back and forth across the rope. His movements were quick and jerky. He was desperate to send the child falling before strangulation could kill him and before the demonic creature on the ground could regain its composure.

Adze got to his feet, ignoring the blistering pain in his face and the agony radiating from his groin. He half stumbled, half ran at LaVelle, intent on tackling the mad priest before he could cut the noose. Adze still hadn't decided what to do with the child, but he didn't intend to let LaVelle carry out his insane ritual.

A huff of breath burst forth from Father LaVelle's mouth as Adze's shoulder blocked him into the wall. The priest gasped and struggled to breathe, the wind having been knocked out of him. Adze, pressing his attack, grabbed a fistful of LaVelle's hair and smashed his face into the brick wall. The first hit broke LaVelle's nose, flooding the priest's mind with pain and blinding him with tears. His cheekbone gave on the second hit and his legs gave out beneath him.

Adze let the priest collapse and turned his attention to the hanging child. The boy was now a deathly shade of blue. It was unclear if he was still alive, and Adze wasn't sure of how to get him down without sending him crashing down the steeple and into the sacrificial pool at its bottom.

He doubted that there was anything to LaVelle's mad ritual, but the clock had passed midnight and Devil's Night had turned to Halloween morning. The veil between worlds was thin, just as LaVelle had raved on about, and Adze didn't want to chance bringing some holy horror—a reborn Christ or otherwise—into the world.

There was the option of leaving the boy to hang, the victim of a single death instead of the three which the ritual seemed to demand, but that didn't sit right with Adze either. The bastard arch-bishop wanted no survivors, but he also hadn't mentioned there were kids involved.

Adze ran out of time to ponder the problem of the child. LaVelle uttered some ancient, unintelligible word behind him. The priest stood up and slashed the weakened rope, sending the boy down the hollow of the stairwell.

Adze dove into the shadows, becoming one with the dark again. He emerged from a blackened corner lower down the stairs and leaped off the edge, catching the falling boy in mid-air. He cradled him as they fell.

LaVelle hung over the railing of the platform above, watching and waiting for the impact. His pulse raced as his great work neared its completion, but his excitement was short-lived. The man-demon and the child passed through a shadow hanging over the sacrificial pool and vanished into its folds.

"No…," Father LaVelle sobbed, collapsing on the ground. "I was so close … so close to saving this city … to saving this world."

Stormclouds began to weep outside, as if in mourning of LaVelle's failure. The wind moaned, crying for the messiah he had failed to resurrect. The orange-gray sky, mottled with black smoke and glowing with the combined sin of all of Detroit, mocked his failure.

The window was closed. At least for another year … or was it? There would be other opportunities—other holy times when he might try again. Christmas was coming, and what better time to resurrect the savior than on the day of his birth? He'd just need another child.

"Just one more," he whispered to himself. "Next time it will work."

"There's no next time, Padre."

LaVelle followed the voice to a shadowed corner and saw two coppery eyes glowing within. Adze stepped out into the dim light. His expression was grave and fierce. It was the face of a man determined to kill.

LaVelle, who was far too hurt to fight back, leaned his head back and cried. He didn't weep for himself, but for the knowledge that his mission would die with him.

The priest held his dagger out in front of him in a moot gesture. Adze kicked it from his hand and picked the priest up by his vestments. He growled and pushed his back into the railing.

"You've ruined everything, you unwholesome monster," LaVelle spat.

"There are three dead kids downstairs … three boys you murdered."

LaVelle began to utter a protest, denying that his actions were murder. Adze slapped him across the face, shutting him up.

"You killed three kids and another may still die. The way I see it, there's only one monster here."

Adze pushed LaVelle over the railing and down the column of space between the stairs. The priest's descent was not smooth. He crashed into the spiraling stairs several times on the way down, bones snapping and limbs dislocating, before splashing into the shallow pool at the bottom.

Exhausted and hurting from the fight and from all the shadow-walking, Adze took his time down the steps. When he finally reached the bottom, he found that LaVelle was still alive, though only by a narrow margin. The priest lay on his back in the puddle of water, gasping and wheezing. His body was a broken mess, all the better to match his mind.

Adze considered leaving him there to suffer a slow death. It was tempting, but he'd been paid to murder the man, and he planned to do just that. He kicked LaVelle onto his stomach, and the priest struggled to keep his face out of the water. He let him fight it for a moment, taking pleasure in his fear and desperation, but Adze soon grew bored with the display. Placing his boot to the back of Father LaVelle's skull, he forced the man's face into the filthy water and held it there until well after he stopped moving.

⁓

"You never said anything about kids," Adze growled, materializing from the corner of the archbishop's bedroom.

Archbishop Edmund Gorecki yelped and shot up in his bed. He reached for the rosary beads on his nightstand and scanned the room. Two familiar coppery eyes glowed in the darkness.

"Is that why you hired me? Because I have no soul or heart? Did you think the Devil's son would have no qualms about killing children?"

The archbishop smoothed out his silk pajama top and flattened down his hair as if he could capture some measure of dignity in the moment.

"How the hell did you get in my home?"

"I came through the nether realm that connects all shadow in this world—the same cold hell where I left that little boy you failed to tell me about. I can bring you there if you like."

"So it's done? LaVelle is dead, along with the children? There are no witnesses?"

"It's done, but the deal has changed. I don't kill kids, as a rule. If I'm forced to break my rules I get twice the pay."

The archbishop huffed in his bed and glared at Adze, though he clutched his rosary beads tighter.

"We had a deal. You'll get what I offered and not a cent more."

"Well, I guess I'll have to make up the cash selling some Polaroids to my pal at the *Detroit Free Press*. Real interesting stuff. I have this one of these three dead little boys laid out around an altar. And then there are these notes that Father LaVelle left behind. I bet the press would pay for those, too. Hell, my reporter friend could probably write a whole book."

⁂

It was Halloween night and Adze sat on the front porch of his house on Abington Avenue, handing out candy to trick-or-treaters. He'd been paid well, all in cash, so he'd decided to splurge and give out full-size Snickers and Twix bars. Word got out, and he found himself with a lot of kids coming around. A few tried to take advantage of him, looping around and coming back. A low growl and a flare in his eyes sent the greedy children scurrying off.

A little after seven o'clock, just when he'd told them to come by, the little boy from the church showed up at his porch, along with his mother. The boy wore a vampire cape that almost covered up the bruising on his neck. His gaze was distant, and he trembled a bit. It would be some time before he got over what LaVelle had put him through.

Adze handed the boy a Snickers and a Twix. The child reluctantly took them. His mother, however, showed no hesitancy at accepting the pillow case stuffed with hundred-dollar bills that Adze gave to her.

"Get of town, and stay away from churches. They'll come for you if they find out he's alive."

The mother backed down the steps, crying and muttering her thanks. As they walked away Adze whispered a prayer of his own—a prayer that devils might protect the boy and his mother from the careless machinations of the devout.

An Angel in Amber Leaves

Martin Novak and Billy Keene arrived at Grand Circus Park well before dawn on the morning of Halloween. Times were tough and the city didn't usually give overtime to folks in the Parks and Recreations department. Halloween was the yearly exception. Folks got rowdy on Devil's Night, and while cops and firefighters dealt with the big stuff, the park department was tasked with the cleanup.

If there was toilet paper on the trees, they took it down. If some punk kids tagged up a statue, they cleaned it. If someone smashed up a bench or a picnic table, they fixed it. There wasn't much glory in what they did for a living, but Martin found meaning in his work and took pride in it. He enjoyed his job and he was thankful for it.

"All right, retard," Billy said, killing the motor to the pickup truck. "Time to make the fucking donuts."

Martin didn't blink at Billy's jab. People had been calling him stupid and slow his whole life, from teachers and classmates to his parents and his co-workers. He'd never been diagnosed with any sort of mental disability, but the general consensus was that he was "a retard." He'd come to accept this without much bitterness.

Being smart didn't seem all that great, anyway. All the folks who lorded their intelligence over him seemed pretty miserable.

He might have had trouble with words and numbers, but he was content, and that seemed to be more than most folks he knew had going for them.

Martin grabbed his thermos from the cup holder, careful not to knock over Billy's Styrofoam cup of coffee. He'd done that a few times, and Billy had blown his top. When Martin helpfully suggested that Billy put his coffee in a thermos so it couldn't spill so easily (adding in the fact that it was cheaper to make coffee at home), his partner went nuclear. He'd shoved him and let out a barrage of curses and insults that made Martin, who assumed everyone made it to church each Sunday, wonder how many Hail Marys the man would need to say after his next confession.

Billy grabbed his own coffee and got out of the truck, groaning about the pre-dawn cold, as he tended to complain about most things. Martin left the truck as well, but the cold didn't bother him. He wore long underwear beneath his jeans and T-shirt, and insulated coveralls over them. A pair of cowhide work gloves hung out of his pocket, and those would be plenty warm for his hands if he needed them.

Despite the cold, and despite the occasional sirens, there was a calm to the morning. The city felt different somehow—a little less mean. Martin wasn't sure what gave him this impression, but he wasn't the type to ponder such things. He just accepted good things as they came to him.

The two men took a moment to scan the area and survey the damage from the night before. Streamers of sopping toilet paper hung from balding trees and clumped on the ground like massive piles of bird shit. Storm-tossed leaves formed mounds at the bases of trees and monuments. Stray beer cans, cigarette butts, and fireworks casings dotted the mud and grass.

"Grab a trash picker and a rake. You can handle the shit on the ground. I'll get the ladder and pull the toilet paper out of the trees," Billy said. "It looks like you already lost a fight with your razor this morning. I don't want you falling off a ladder."

Martin ran his fingers across his neck in a self-conscious gesture. He shaved every morning, and every morning he cut himself and missed some spots. For some reason he just couldn't get the knack of it.

Billy wasn't Martin's boss. He didn't even have seniority over him, but Martin didn't care. If it made Billy happy to call the shots, so be it. He wasn't concerned about what he was doing anyway, so long as it meant he was busy and useful.

Martin pulled a trash bag off a roll in the bed of the pickup and shook it open before putting on his gloves. Three needle-pointed trashpickers sat in the bed of the truck and Martin examined the tip on each. Billy huffed behind him, but Martin ignored him and focused on determining which was the sharpest. Once he was satisfied that he'd made the right choice, Martin turned toward the park, plastic bag in one hand, trashpicker in the other.

"You forgot the rake!" Billy hollered.

"One thing at a time a time." Martin's words, as always, were slow and drawn out. Folks sometimes called him Eeyore when he spoke, which he never found insulting.

Billy huffed but let the matter drop. Despite how he acted, he also knew that he wasn't actually the boss.

The ground was littered with all manner of debris. Some if it had blown out of trashcans or down side streets during the storm last night, but Martin guessed that a lot of the mess was people's carelessness. No one seemed to care much about the city, aside from the folks who took care of it—the cops, paramedics, and firefighters. Martin liked to count himself in their ranks. He wasn't saving lives, but he was still a public servant doing what he could to take care of the city.

Martin stabbed at the litter and filled his trashbag with empty pop cans and Styrofoam Big Mac containers. He bent down for the stuff that he couldn't pierce with the trashpicker—a shattered beer bottle here, a used syringe there. Someone had smashed a few pumpkins in the grass as well, but he left those for later. They'd get tossed in with the the yard waste when he raked.

He ignored the piles of wet leaves for now, unless there was obvious litter mixed in with them. When he saw a bottle or can sticking up from the dead foliage he'd snatch it up and save himself the trouble of separating it later. A large bed of amber and carnelian leaves had gathered below a massive tree in the middle of the park, and a rusted piece of rebar jutted out from it. It was so close in color to the leaves that Martin had almost missed it, but for some reason it caught his eye, even in the dim pre-dawn.

Martin stabbed his garbage picker into the ground and knelt to pick up the length of rebar. He felt something hard and lumpy below the leaves, but he wrote it off as tree roots. Grabbing the rebar, Martin found that it was stuck. Some bored teenagers had probably pounded it into the roots or deep into the dirt. He pulled harder and the metal rod released with a wet slurping noise.

The jagged end of the rebar was coated in dark ooze. In the shadows of the big tree, sheltered from the street lights, the viscous liquid looked black as night. Martin wondered if it was oil, but could not guess what kind of tree produced black oil when you stabbed it.

He cleared away the wet autumnal foliage and his breath caught in his chest. A still woman stared up at him from the bed of leaves. Long red hair hung about hair head in fiery halo, as if she floated on water. Her blue eyes, almost as crystalline pale as her flesh, stared unmoving toward the sky.

To call her movie-star gorgeous would be like comparing the sun to a candle's flame. She was the most beautiful thing he had ever seen.

She was nearly naked, dressed only in a torn, wet T-shirt that clung to her curves. An ugly wound, black and wet, seeped in the center of her chest. The same dark, viscous gore that coated the rusted rebar stained the white concert shirt she wore, blotting out half of Debbie Harry's face.

The woman's chest did not rise or fall. Martin pressed his fingers to her neck to feel for a pulse, the way he'd seen it done on *Trapper John, M.D.* and *St. Elsewhere*. He felt nothing.

Panic gripped Martin's heart and he looked around for someone to help—someone smart. There were no cruisers parked nearby, and no ambulances driving down the dark, lonely street. Billy was here, though. He was a jerk, but he'd know what to do.

Martin scanned the area and saw his colleague cutting away the innards of a cassette tape that were wrapped around a bronze head of a statue across the park. He leaned over the woman who he feared was dead and tried to give her a reassuring look.

"I'm gonna get help," he said, speaking even slower than usual.

Martin went to turn away from her—to run off and get Billy—but he found himself paralyzed by the woman's icy gaze. He could almost hear her voice in his mind begging him not to leave her.

Don't leave me. They'll put me in the ground and you'll never see me again.

Minutes earlier Martin had not known that beauty such as hers even existed. Now the thought of losing her to the cold, consuming earth was too much to bear. He was in love with her, not the way that men and women fall in love with each other, but in the way that one falls in love with the divine. He didn't want to possess this woman; he wanted to serve her. He didn't desire her in a carnal fashion, any more than he desired to make love to a sunset or the night sky. She was just as far beyond him as those things were.

Martin pulled a second trashbag from his belt and unfolded it. He laid it across the woman in the leaves—the angel in the leaves—granting her a measure of warmth and modesty. He cursed the slow gears of his mind as he struggled for some idea of what to do. How could he help her without risking them taking her away?

Take me home.

The words, a feminine whisper in his mind, sounded real. There was a weight to them, and he could almost feel the breath that spoke them against his ear.

Billy was still wrestling with endless yards of Memorex guts. He paid Martin no mind.

Martin was almost afraid to touch her, afraid that his skin might burn at her touch or that she might scream and claw at him for placing his crude, calloused hands upon her.

It's okay.

Martin's hands shook as he placed his arms beneath the woman's head and under her knees. Her skin did not burn him. It was as if she were carved from ice—smooth and freezing cold. He lifted her from the ground as gently as he could manage, careful to keep her blanketed beneath the trashbag. He held her tight to his chest and carried her to the pickup truck.

Her head lolled toward him, her face nuzzling in the crook of his neck. Her lips pressed against his skin, cold and wet from the rain. For a moment Martin thought she was kissing his throat, but then it was over, and he questioned if it had happened at all.

The thought of putting her in the bed of the truck was revolting to Martin. It was a place for trash and rusted tools. But he had little choice. If he put her in the front seat someone would see her, and they'd think she was dead. They'd take her away from him.

Laying her down in the bed of the pickup, Martin apologized and promised that she wouldn't have to stay there long. He stared into her unblinking eyes, hoping to see some glint of understanding—hoping to see that she wasn't angry at him for the indignity. Her gaze showed no expression.

The black horizon turned blue between the buildings. Sunrise approached and a terrible thought struck Martin's mind with the speed and ferocity of a lightning strike. The sun, for all its radiance, would be jealous of his angel's beauty. It would try to destroy her. He knew this with the same conviction that he knew he had to eat each day and that something tossed in the air falls to the ground.

Martin took the black trashbag and opened it up. He slid it over his angel's legs and up to her navel, careful not to touch her inappropriately or with lack of proper respect. He apologized once more before pulling a second trash bag over her head and shoulders, down to her waist. He hated to inflict such indignity upon her, but now she was protected from the envious sun.

Billy had left the keys in the ignition of the truck. Martin had always thought that was an irresponsible habit, but now he was grateful of it. The starter of the truck wheezed for a moment before the motor turned over with a growl. Martin shifted into drive and pulled away from the park. He could hear Billy yelling, and he could see him in the rearview, chasing after him. A guilty smirk crossed his lips.

Martin's headlights shone into the darkness and reflected off the wet asphalt. The smoky haze of Devil's Night and the acrid smell of mass arson had been washed away by the storm that had raged overnight, and the lunatics and hoodlums who had set fire to the city had finally crawled back into their holes. The sky was a proper midnight blue, instead of a hazy mess of grayish orange. A sense of peace had fallen across the land, only broken here and there by the stray siren or car alarm.

The road ahead of him was flat, as was most of Michigan, and up ahead he could see the very line where the luxury architecture of the financial district gave way to squalor. One block was all glass, brass, and stone marked with plaques bearing the names of lawyers and brokers. The next was shuttered storefronts tagged with gang symbols to mark out territory and drug spots.

By the time Martin had pulled up to his house, a single-family on the southwest side of the city, the sun had crested the horizon. Normally Martin liked this time of day. The good and honest folks of the city did their business now, while the crooks and the bad guys slept in.

Old Miss Williams was coming out of her house to walk Matilida, her old lady dog. A group of kids were playing on the sidewalk, dressed in winter coats and plastic monster masks. Jane from next door was getting home from an overnight shift at the diner so she could get a few hours of shuteye before clocking in for her mid-morning shift at the drycleaner.

Martin locked up the truck and opened the tailgate. He didn't dare drag the angel out as if she were some piece of refuse, so he climbed into the back and lifted her in his arms, careful not to let the trashbags slip and expose her skin. He crouched down with her then butt-scooted off the tailgate, not bothering to close it after.

An Angel in Amber Leaves

Wet leaves covered the steps to Martin's front door. He made sure not to slip on them as he tried to retrieve his house keys without dropping the angel.

"You need a hand, Martin?" a voice called out from behind him.

Old Miss Williams was coming his way. Matilda was lagging behind, pulling back on her leash. Martin smiled and assured Miss Williams that he had everything under control.

"Oh, you don't need to be all macho with me, Martin. I can see you struggling. Let me get the door for you."

Matilda continued pulling back on her leash, whimpering the whole time. Miss Williams told the old mutt to stop being such a baby, but the dog wouldn't listen.

"Fine, stay there," she said, placing the handle of Matilda's leash over the top of a fire hydrant. "I have no clue what's got into that old gal."

Matilda barked like mad as Miss Williams walked up the steps to Martin's front door. She shushed the dog and took the keys from Martin's hand with a warm smile. He smiled back, terrified that his nervousness would show through.

"Which key is it, dear?"

"The brass one," he replied. "The one that's shaped like the Chrysler symbol on top."

Martin moved aside so that his neighbor could open the door for him. He prayed she wouldn't ask about the bundle he carried, or try to peak beneath the plastic.

"Looks like you're carrying a dead body." She laughed at her own joke as she fiddled with the lock.

"The things you find in this city," he droned in his slow deadpan.

Miss Williams broke into laughter again. She swung the door open and patted Martin on the shoulder, wishing him a pleasant day. As he stepped inside, he could hear the old woman reprimanding her barking dog. Martin shut the door with his foot and headed straight for his bedroom.

Sunlight crept in through the gap between the shades and the window frame, painting thin lines across the threadbare carpet and across his neatly made twin bed. Martin placed his bundle onto the bed with a sense of gentle reverence. He so badly wanted to free the angel from the black plastic she was cocooned in, but he needed to block up the windows first or the jealous sun would set her aflame.

"I'll be right back," he said.

Martin retrieved a roll of trashbags from under the kitchen sink and a box of thumbtacks from a junk drawer. The bags weren't as heavy as the ones that he had wrapped his angel in, but they were black and opaque and would do the job. He returned to his room and cut the kitchen bags into long sheets, then tacked them over the window frame to block out the narrow beams of sunlight.

He closed his bedroom door and found himself in complete darkness, save for the slivers of light that snuck under the door from the hallway. That little bit of radiance wasn't a concern. It barely made it past the threshold and did not come anywhere close to his bed. Satisfied that the envious sun posed no immediate threat, Martin flipped on his light switch and walked over to his bed.

He pulled away the top bag, and his angel's hair clung to the plastic. Her locks fell to the bed as the static electricity lost its grip. Her red mane, littered with amber leaves, reminded him once more of a fiery halo. He pulled the second trashbag away from her lower body and folded both in case he needed to cover her again.

In the dim pre-dawn he had assumed that the dark gore which stained her shirt and filled the hole in her chest was blood, but under proper lighting Martin could see no red tint to it. It was thick and black, like molasses, but stank of rot and death. He wondered if that was how angels bled, or if there had been something poisonous on that jagged rebar she'd been stabbed with.

Martin stared into her unblinking eyes and wondered who would do such a thing. What kind of monster would try to destroy such a beautiful creature? Whatever their motives, he was by her side now and he wouldn't let her die.

He didn't need to ask her how to help. She spoke to him without words. Their shared gaze communicated all that Martin needed to know.

"I'll be right back," he promised, covering her with a quilt that lay folded at the bottom of his bed.

Martin went to the bathroom and turned the hot-water faucet all the way up. He grabbed a cleaning bucket from under the sink and took several face cloths from the closet as the water warmed. When he returned to fill the bucket with hot water, Martin caught his own reflection in the mirror of the medicine cabinet. His neck, raw and red with tiny nicks from shaving this morning, was now smooth where the angel's lips had pressed against him. He ran a finger across the spot and felt no irritation. He smiled, now sure that he had not imagined her kiss.

White tendrils of steam rose from the bucket as Martin carried it back into his bedroom. It was nearly as cold in the house as it was outside, and Martin refused to turn on the thermostat until November, so the heat rising from the water felt nice. He hoped it would feel as nice to her.

Once he had closed the door behind him, Martin placed the bucket on the floor and dropped one of the face cloths into the steaming water. He knelt down next to his bed and unsheathed a Swiss Army knife from his belt, the same one he'd had since he was fourteen. The scissors opened with ease, despite the age of the tool. *Take good care of your tools and your tools will take good care of you*—that was one of his favorite adages.

Martin cut along the sides of the angel's gore-stained concert shirt, careful not to nick her. The shirt made a wet, slurping sound as he peeled it from her chest. Few things could unsettle Martin. He regularly scraped dead animals from the road and picked up syringes and condoms from the ground. The sludge that had oozed out of the angel's wound and onto her shirt bothered him no more than anything in his daily routine might. He tossed the T-shirt scrap into a waste basket by his bed, just as he might discard a used tissue.

The face cloth steamed as he rang it out over the bucket. Its warmth felt good on his hands. He stood up and approached the angel with the wet cloth.

"I'll get you cleaned up all nice," he said, staring into her eyes, careful not to let his gaze fall to her naked, gore-stained chest. "No funny business. I promise."

Martin gently scrubbed her face. Layers of filth and grime dissolved under the hot water of the face cloth. Beneath the dirt, her cheeks were the color of moonlight and her lips were almost blue—a stark contrast to her fiery hair.

He rinsed the face cloth and washed her neck and shoulders until he got to her chest and the vicious wound between her breasts. He blushed, afraid to look directly at her exposed flesh.

It's okay to look. It's okay to touch.

Her voice rang in Martin's mind, reassuring him and alleviating his anxiety. He ran the wet fabric across the arch of her breast, acutely aware of the soft curving skin that was only separated from his own by a sliver of cotton. A nervous shudder overcame him as his hand passed over her erect nipple. Shame and excitement flooded his mind.

It's okay.

Martin had never touched a woman before, not in this way. He had never kissed anyone, and his hands had never explored the curves and dimensions of the female form. It wasn't that he didn't desire women; he was just dumb and ugly. He didn't deserve a woman. Everyone he had ever known had told him as much, though some had done so with more tact than others.

The angel did not shun him or shame him the way everyone else in his life had. She spoke to him with soft kindness and invited his touch. He took time and care cleaning the black mess from her chest. When he was done he stood over her and looked down at her the perfect mounds of her chest and the angry black hole between her breasts. The skin around the wound was ragged and dark. It looked dead, almost frostbitten.

"I'm gonna clean that out," Martin droned. "It might hurt a little."

Martin soaked a fresh face cloth, then wrung it out. He leaned over the angel and dabbed the cloth against the hole in her chest.

She didn't flinch or cry out in pain, so he began wipe at the wound. Traces of black sludge came up with each soft stroke of the face cloth.

Eventually, Martin wiped away all the surface mess and found that the dark liquid had congealed deeper in the wound. He pulled out his Swiss Army knife again, this time sliding a pair of stainless steel tweezers from the handle. He gripped the edge of the black clot in her chest and muttered an apology as he tugged at it.

A violent tremor shuddered through the angel's body as Martin ripped the clot from her wound. Thin tendrils of smoke rose from the hole in her chest and a smell like charred pork filled the room.

Martin shot back, dropping the tweezers and the congealed gore onto the carpet. He mumbled repeated apologies before leaning over her again. He looked for some sign of anger or pain in her eyes. He looked for some sign of disappointment or hate. There was nothing but heaven in her cool blue eyes, however.

Keep going.

Martin nodded in compliance to the voice in his head. He knelt down to grab the tweezers and found that the clotted gore still hung from them. Flakes of rust speckled the black sludge—remnants of the rebar the angel had been stabbed with. He wiped the tweezers on the edge of his waste basket and stood up.

With the big clot gone, Martin could see that tiny bits of rusted iron were lodged in the angel's exposed tissue. The iron was poisoning her. He was no doctor, nor an expert on the nature of angels, but he knew this the same way he knew that the sun would destroy her.

Tiny trails of smoke rose up with each piece of rust he removed from her chest. Her body spasmed in short bursts and her lips curled, exposing teeth like ivory daggers—teeth crafted for tearing apart the mean and sinful.

It took some time, but Martin removed all the flakes of rust and splinters of iron that he could find from the angel's wound. Her lips relaxed back into a look of non-expression. Her gaze never wavered from the ceiling.

A knock echoed through the house. No, not a knock—a pounding. Someone was battering his front door.

Martin covered the angel with his quilt and assured her he would be right back.

Someone was yelling between the banging. The voice was so loud and raw that he couldn't place it until it screamed, "Open up, retard!"

It was Billy, of course. Martin had taken the truck and left him back at the park. Now he was pissed.

Martin stood still and held his breath. Maybe he could just pretend he wasn't home and Billy would go away.

"I know you're home, Martin! The truck's right out front!"

"Shit," Martin whispered to himself.

He tried to come up with excuses for taking off with the truck, but his thoughts were a slippery, jumbled mess. This happened to him a lot, pretty much whenever he tried to think too hard. It was one of the reasons he avoided lying.

"One minute!" Martin shouted.

He reluctantly shuffled toward the door, with no idea what he was going to say once he opened it. He wondered if Billy was going to tell on him and get him in trouble at work. He wondered if he would sock him in the mouth for leaving him behind.

Martin's hand trembled as he turned the lock on the knob. As soon as he opened the door, Billy pushed his way into the house.

"You think you're fucking funny driving off without me? Huh, retard?"

"I ... um ..."

"Uh ... um ... duh," Billy mocked.

"I'm sorry, Billy."

"I saw you throw something in the back of the truck before you took off. You find some money? Drugs?"

"I didn't find anything." The lie stung to say. He *had* found something. He had found the most beautiful thing in all the world.

"Oh, yeah? You wanna hold out on me?" Billy asked. "I wonder what the boss will say when I tell him you left your partner behind and went AWOL. I wonder what he'll say when I tell him you stole a city truck. That's a felony, Martin!"

Panic gripped Martin's mind, so much that he didn't even realize that Billy was shoving him further into the house. He didn't want to lose his job. He didn't want to go to jail.

"No, no, no, Billy!" Martin pleaded. "Please don't tell!"

Billy eased up. He stopped pushing Martin and took on a pose of faux thoughtfulness. "Well maybe we could put this behind us, if you could make it worth my while. Say if you found something of value in the park? I wouldn't even be greedy. I'd let you keep thirty percent."

Martin's gaze shifted over to his bedroom door, then back to Billy. He swallowed hard and shook his head.

Billy smiled. "It's in there? What is it? Cash? Coke?"

"I didn't find anything. I just came home because I didn't feel good."

"You can't lie for shit." Billy shoved Martin into the wall. He stormed past him and into the bedroom.

Martin recovered his balance and ran after his co-worker.

"What the fuck is this?" Billy asked, shifting his eyes from the bucket of brackish water and the soiled face cloths to the huddled, covered mass on the bed.

"Please, Billy, just leave."

Billy did not listen. He tossed aside the quilt and stared in shock at the lifeless, naked woman with a hole in her chest. A look of horror overtook his face, followed by an expression of disgust.

"You sick motherfucker."

Billy turned away from the body before he could see the woman's dead skin begin to blister and burn at the touch of the sunlight stretching in through the open doorway. He shoved Martin into the wall and pressed his forearm against his throat.

"This is what gets you off, retard? Oh, your pervy ass is so going to jail."

Stars exploded in front of Martin's eyes as Billy choked him out against the wall. He struggled and tried to push back, but he wasn't strong enough. If it was just his life at stake, he might have just given in to unconsciousness, but this was bigger than him.

The angel began to seize on his bed. She was in pain. She was in danger. He had to help.

Seeing no other choice, Martin reached down for his Swiss Army knife and thumbed open the knife blade. He plunged it into Billy's side, just below the ribs. Billy's arm slackened and Martin sucked in a gasp of air. The knife slid out and blood gushed from Billy's torso, covering Martin's hand like a crimson glove. Martin stabbed him twice more, then pushed him to the ground.

Curses and moans rolled off Billy's lips as he pressed down on his wounds. Martin was reminded of the little Dutch boy trying to plug the dam with his finger. He didn't take much time to dwell on the thought, though. Instead, he rushed for the bedroom door and closed it, sparing his angel from the sun's assault.

"I'm so sorry," Martin whispered.

"Sorry? You stabbed me, you maniac!"

"I wasn't talking to you."

The smoldering corpse—the burning angel—sat up. A slow wheezing escaped her lungs as she crawled down from the bed, like some sort of predatory cat. Billy screamed as she smiled at him with a razorblade grin.

The angel pounced onto Billy and bit into his already wounded side. She tore through his flesh with those teeth made to purge the mean and wicked and slurped at his insides. He thrashed and howled until his body gave out.

Martin watched all this, not in horror, but relief. Even as the angel devoured his co-worker—as she snapped his bones and sucked out the marrow—her burns gave way to smooth, unmarred skin. She was going to be okay.

It didn't take long for the angel to finish her meal. In a matter of minutes she had consumed all Billy's blood and innards, leaving only a ragged skin bag filled with gristle and broken bones. She stood up once she was done, unsteady on her feet.

A glaze of gore covered most of her body, but the skin that

shown through now had a warmth to its complexion. The hole in her chest was mostly healed. Only a shallow red indent remained.

As healthy as she looked, the angel stumbled and Martin rushed to hold her up. She leaned on him, pressing her body against his. Martin asked if she was all right. He asked what else he might do for her?

She looked into his eyes and spoke without speaking.

※

The rancid smell of the city dump wafted into the truck, despite the windows being rolled up. Martin didn't mind the stink too much. It was better than the smell of Devil's Night—that toxic campfire smell of burning wood and melting siding. Anyway, he was used to dealing with nastiness. You couldn't be a public servant in Detroit without getting dirty.

Martin got out of the truck and unloaded the bags from the back. Most of them were filled with trash he'd picked up in the parks and off the sidewalks. One of the bags held his personal garbage, though. He wasn't supposed to dump his own waste in the dump, but this was a special circumstance.

Bones clacked together as the trashbag hit the mound of waste. No one was around to hear the noise or to worry about it, save for the rats.

Martin got back into the truck and left the garbage dump. He wasn't sure if it was in his head, but the city felt different. It felt brighter and less claustrophobic. He swore that he could feel a change in the air. Maybe the fires or the storm from the night before had purged some great evil. Or maybe he was just in love.

It was crazy to think that he had known the angel for less than a day and already she had changed his life forever. He was thankful that she was getting better, but she wasn't fully healed. She needed to rest. She needed to feed.

He scanned the streets as he drove, like an owl hunting for mice. He ignored the hordes of trick-or-treaters and the teenagers roughhousing in the street. He searched for someone mean and sinful—someone who might not be missed.

Martin was no hero. He wasn't a cop or a firefighter, but he was good at the dirty jobs others didn't want. He had been a public servant for most of his life. Now he was a servant of a different kind.

The Exorcism of Detroit, Michigan

Y'a'll want a written confession? Ya'll want me to say I'm a maniac or a terrorist? Maybe even a Satanist? That would make for good headlines—*DETROIT POLICE APPREHEND SATANIC TERRORIST*. The mayor could hide all his failures behind a smokescreen like that for months. Everybody would be looking for pentagrams and upside-down crosses instead of graffiti marking out gang turf and spots to score crack.

It's not like that, though. The truth is I saved this city, when no one else could, or when no one else would, at least.

That probably burns your asses—the thought of some middle-aged Black woman, especially a Black woman who looks more Florida Evans than Grace Jones, locking shit down while all you macho men in blue play cops and robbers with teenage gangbangers.

Don't blame yourselves, though, boys. I have a certain skill set that I was born into—insights and attunements you couldn't imitate with a lifetime of practice. It's like the saying goes: you either got it or you don't, honey.

So no, I won't confess to terrorism or public endangerment, or any of the bullshit charges being thrown at me. Maybe the murder charge, though I wouldn't call it that. Calling it murder is like charging a Marine for the VCs he shot in 'Nam. War is its own thing, you know?

I will confess to the truth, however, not that I suspect you'll believe it. I can't imagine you'd be capable of believing what really happened out by the Detroit River on October 30th. A small part of me is envious of that ignorance.

To understand what happened last night, you need to understand who I am. My name ain't important, but I was born here in Detroit in the summer of 1940. My daddy was a *bokor*, or a Voodoo sorcerer if you'd rather. He came here from Louisiana and met my mama, who was a palm reader and a fortune teller. Truth be told, Mama was a fraud. She was real good at reading folks and telling them what they wanted to hear, but that was the extent of her clairvoyance.

My daddy, though—he was the real thing. Daddy came from a long line of Voodoo folk, going back to our ancestors in Haiti, and he was skilled in all aspects of the art. You probably think that means he spent his time stabbing pins into dolls and divining the future with chicken bones, and you'd be partially right, but his skills went so much deeper.

You'd never know that Daddy was a *bokor*. He owned three tidy suits and hardly any other clothes. They were nothing flashy or expensive, but they were respectable outfits that he took great pride in. To look at him you might guess he was a professor or a librarian, not that there were many Black men in those professions back then.

He rarely messed around with shit like B-movie curses, and I never saw him raise the dead, but when we needed a bit of money or luck, he had a knack for magicking it up. And if someone needed help with love or life, something beyond what Mama could offer with her bullshit psychic routine, and if they had the cheddar, Daddy would step in and make things right for them.

I suspect that my own talents came from him. As far back as I can remember I was able to commune with the city itself. I could hear the thoughts of the rats and the roaches. I could close my eyes and see through the eyes of the birds and hear a hundred discordant voices chattering across telephone cables. The TV static revealed secrets to me, both beautiful and terrifying, just the way scattered bones did for Daddy.

As I got older my gifts became more pronounced. I've never once been lost in my whole life. No matter where I ended up in the city, the streets would point the way home. If I ended up in a place I shouldn't be, the city would hide me from any dangers. It was like I was invisible to the gangbangers, the perverts, and even the police. And if I did get into trouble, as young girls who grow up in rough neighborhoods often do, the living spirit of Detroit would come to my aid in the form of swarming alley cats or some equally strange phenomenon. You ain't never seen anything so funny as some wannabe gangster running away screaming while two dozen tomcats run him down.

Daddy said I was connected to the city's Loa—the spirit of Detroit itself. He said I was special—that I had a gift. I'd come to learn that other cultures throughout history had parallels—folks who were in tune with the spirit of their home. The Celts called them druids and dryads. Injuns have their shamans. The Vikings knew them as *vǫlur*. Once Christianity took hold they were all lumped together as witches.

Whatever you want to call me—a witch or a Satanist or what the hell ever—it don't matter. Just so long as you get the point. I can talk to the streets and the streets can talk to me.

Now like I said, there are some perks that come with this sort of spiritual connection to the city, but it ain't all roses. I can feel when it's hurting. I can feel when it's sick. And let's face it, Detroit's been in pain for most of my life, and probably long before. There's a darkness here—a darkness that sucks up joy and love and spits out black anger.

I used to think that was just the dark side of the city. I chalked it up to the duality of all things—yin and yang and all that—but I'd come to realize that it was something else altogether. There is a parasite wrapped around the heart of this city—or rather there was, until last night—an evil and ancient thing that was born way before crack and heroin poisoned the streets or Henry Ford's newspaper poisoned people's minds. It had burrowed into the soil long before White fur trappers or Black slaves walked the land and even before the Potawatomi settled here.

Not to say that this place wouldn't have a dark side otherwise, but I can't imagine it would be so pronounced. All titanic things cast a shadow, and Detroit is no different. Even now that it's been freed from its parasitic possession, who knows if things will get better? It will take time for the city to heal of course, if it even can at this point. The parasite is dead and time will tell.

Sorry, I'm getting ahead of myself. Before I can get into the evil thing that was warping the heart of our city, I need to tell you about my husband. Understanding Charles (I refuse to call him by his ridiculous made-up Black Power name) is as key to grasping what went down on Devil's Night as understanding me is.

I first met Charles in the summer of 1962. The Summer of Love was years away and Jimi Hendrix was still in the army, so Charles was the first hippie I'd ever seen. His hair was an unkempt Afro and his outfit was a thrift store rock-'n'-roll ensemble made up of rainbow scarves, washed-out denim, and an unbuttoned blouse that looked as if he'd stolen it from some Shakespearean dressing room.

I have to admit, I was intrigued by that gypsy vagabond look, but it was his strong jaw and those fierce brown eyes that gave me butterflies. Life and passion burned behind his gaze with an intensity I had never seen. It was beautiful, inspiring, and a little bit terrifying. He'd later tell me that he saw the same intensity in my own eyes, which I guess makes sense. We were both cut from the same cloth, so to speak. We were destined to be lovers, I suppose, just as we were destined to be enemies.

How did we even discover that we shared the same kind of connection to the spirit of the city? I couldn't tell you. There was no grand moment of revelation. I don't think that we even talked about it at first. We just knew.

Daddy didn't like Charles from the get-go. He didn't approve of his messy hair or his hippie clothes. He hated the way he talked and the relaxed, arrogant swagger of his walk. I remember him saying that Black men couldn't afford to be weird the way White folks could. He thought Charles was asking for trouble, and that I was going to get caught up in it along with him.

"You can be whoever the hell you want behind closed doors," he'd say, pointing out his shelf of herbs and tinctures. "But don't give the outside world any more reason to dislike you than you're already burdened with."

Mama, on the other hand, liked Charles just fine. I think she always dreamed of a nomadic carnival lifestyle, fleecing folks as a traveling palm reader or some such thing. She saw in Charles the sort of free spirit she wished she could have been. It didn't hurt that he was charming and handsome.

Charles and I had a whirlwind love affair and we married just after a year. Being around each other, exploring each other's bodies and minds, led us to a greater mastery over our powers and strengthened our connections to the city. We became stronger together, but in turn our vision sharpened and we began to see more and more of the evil all around us. We both felt that black, hateful venom coursing through the tree roots and the power lines, though neither of us knew what it was at the time.

Detroit is a haunted town, full of ghosts and legends, but there are more spirits here than even the superstitious might think. When enough power and energy is siphoned into a thing, when enough life is sacrificed to it, it can grow a spirit all its own. Detroit is full of such beings. Some of them go back to days of the Injuns—beings like the Snake Goddess of Belle Isle.

Others are younger. There's the demigod of the auto industry, a spirit who looks the way you might picture the ghost of Henry Ford. He smells of grease and gasoline and brings both prosperity and death. Drug demons—imps with venomous syringes jutting out from their fingertips and breath that stinks with the burning plastic smell of crack cocaine, stalk the playgrounds, the projects, and the trailer parks. The twin god and goddess of Motown—

the souls of soul—breathe in love, heartbreak, hope, and misery before each soothing note they sing into the night.

We began to see ourselves as stewards of Detroit—its servants and guardians. Charles and I would make offerings to the beneficial spirits of the city. We'd make love while the Supremes played on the record player, offering our love and lust to the spirits of Motown. When shades would form—that's what we took to calling a spirit birthed from the combined pain and hate of numerous tragedies occurring at a single spot over time—we would banish or destroy them.

Shades are an important part of this story. When we were young we thought we had them all figured out. They always formed at epicenters of tragedy. Whorehouses filled with doped-up little girls. Projects where too many mothers lost their sons to guns and drugs. Junkyards and basements that hosted dog fights and underground boxing. The locations where they were birthed varied, but it was always a physical place, so we somehow missed the shade that was gestating within Charles himself.

My husband, when I met him, was a free spirit who was rarely seen without a smile on his face. He was jovial despite his circumstances, not because of them. His mama was a hellfire-and-brimstone Christian, and being an unwed mother never seemed to complicate that for her. Unlike my Voodoo daddy and psychic fraud momma, Charles's mother saw his gifts as a curse. She said he had the devil in his heart and she tried to beat it out of him on a regular basis. He ran away when he was fifteen and never looked back.

It wasn't just his mama that made things hard for Charles either. He was too sensitive and too trusting. He'd let people in and they'd hurt him. Throughout his teenage years, he'd made friends with a few older men, surrogate father figures, all of whom tried to take advantage of him in one way or another once he'd dropped his guard.

He'd seen the friends he made on the street picked off one by one. Sometimes it was drugs. Other times it was the cold and malnutrition. Occasionally it was the cops or the gangs.

And then there was the girl who came before me. I don't like to think about that much, my husband with another woman, but people have lives before you meet them, and you can't own another human being. Charles got this other woman pregnant. Even though they were young and had a troubled relationship, he'd been beyond excited for the baby, but that child never made it into the world. This other woman got caught up in drugs, heroin mostly, and she lost the baby. That crushed Charles. We only talked about it once, and it was one of the few times I ever saw my husband cry.

And of course, there were the tragedies not his own that he could feel through his connection to the soul of the city. These seemed to affect him worse than any of his personal losses. I've learned to tune out a lot of that noise—the pain and suffering of my neighbors. I'm ashamed to admit that, but if you don't you'll go mad. All that tragedy will build up inside you until it overtakes you—until a shade is born in your soul.

I think the turning point for Charles was the year following the riots in '68. The city was in such turmoil and it was going through so much change. He started getting angry after that. He was pissed at the Black folks for looting and burning, pissed at the cops for their violence against the people they were supposed to protect, and pissed at the White folks for turning their back on the city he loved so much.

Charles hadn't lost himself to the darkness yet, though you could see the hardness in his soul starting to form whenever you looked him in the eyes. Despite all that, we still did good work in those closing years of the '60s. After White flight, a lot the grocery stores shut down and it became hard even to get decent food in some neighborhoods. Charles saw this and took up an interest in botany and urban farming. He could talk to the earth and coax life from it, even from the tough, barren soil in the city.

Despite the good we were doing, my husband's heart grew colder with each passing dawn. Negative vibes resonated from every street corner in those days. Jobs were drying up in the auto plants. Everybody had less money—except the drug dealers, who were doing better than ever. And while Detroit had always been broken up into tribes of sorts, racial tensions were higher than ever with Birchers and trailer-park Nazis stoking the fires on one side and the Nation of Islam and the Black Panthers on the other.

Now, I never cared much about race. I figured my connection to the city was deeper than the flesh. It was something I shared with the native shamans who walked this ground before me, and an adjacent experience to what red-headed White folk dancing around Stonehenge might have felt. The spirit knows no color, you know?

Charles didn't feel that way anymore. He felt betrayed by the way so many had abandoned the city and left it to economic ruin and urban decay. He said that if the White folks wanted to flee to the suburbs then they had no right to the city proper. There was, for him, no more empathic connection to the various tribes of Detroit, Michigan, and he began to see his role as an architect rather than a steward.

This is around the time that Charles and I ran into marital trouble. By 1970 he had cut his hair short and traded in his hippie digs for some three-piece suits—the kind of stuff my daddy used to wear. The time for free spirits had come and gone, he'd said. "Today calls for stern men of action." I think those were his words.

Evidently what that meant was running drugs and guns, and then soliciting children to do those things for him. When I asked him how he could betray our community like that, how he could pump poison and death into the city we loved, he explained that crime and vice couldn't be eliminated, so they had to be controlled. As far as Charles was concerned, he was the only man capable of managing such things.

It wasn't just the amateur kingpin shit that marked such a change in him either. He started hanging around those Nation of Islam cats, cherry-picking their religion, even though he was connected to the divine so much deeper than any of those men could ever understand. Once that hit a dead end he moved on to that five-percenter shit—that stuff too kooky for the Nation of

Islam. You know who I'm talking about, the dudes who holler in the park about the Asiatic Black man being God? Well, Charles ate that shit up.

His whole worldview became filtered through those ideas. He claimed that was why he and I had the powers and the insights that we did. He started calling himself DOR, some goofy acronym taken from their corny ass "Supreme Alphabet" and referring to our city as D-Mecca. He would rant about how it was our duty to shape the character of the city.

Charles might have fallen for that five-percenter scam, but he was smart, and despite the darkness growing within him, his connection to the city was incredibly strong. He could make it bend to his will in ways you wouldn't believe. He could have been the shadow king of this city, ruling behind the scenes. I can't imagine anything could have stopped him in those years of chaos and decay. I loved him so much I might have followed him down that path. The passion of a handsome man can be a powerful current to get swept along in, especially if that passion comes with money and power. But Charles's path diverged once again, down even darker roads.

Somewhere along the line, Charles started viewing himself as a literal god. He said if there was a creator in the sky, it was not the god of the Black man, or else he'd not have given us such a tough lot in life. Thus, he saw it as his role, given his special gifts, to serve as the patron deity of Detroit, Michigan, and reshape the city in his image. To do so, however, the whole thing had to be torn down and burned to the ground—a sacrifice of the city to the city.

By the time the first real Devil's Night occurred, that first year when it turned from teenage vandalism to widescale arson, I'd already left Charles. I hadn't spoken to him in months, but I knew he was behind it. Every flame I saw that night glowed with my husband's aura. I could see Charles's passion and rage behind the eyes of every crazed teenager. I don't how he did it—how he became so strong—but my husband was no longer communing with the city. He had possessed it.

The Exorcism of Detroit, Michigan

No, scratch that. A shade, the same one that had latched on to my husband's soul, possessed the city. That evil parasite used Charles and manipulated his gifts. It made a mockery of him.

In the following years, I tried to save my husband. I tried to banish the monstrous thing that had grown inside his soul, with my words as well as my gifts. I wasn't strong enough. Love always wins out in the storybooks and the big Hollywood pictures, but real life ain't like that, baby.

When it became clear that I couldn't save my husband, I decided to save the city from him. So there you go, you have your premeditation on record. I sure as hell planned on killing Charles. It was the only way.

Last night, while everyone else was looking up at the smoke in the sky, the black venomous roots beneath this city were supping upon the fear, anger, and hatred that Devil's Night elicits. They stretch from the tips of the suburbs, and a fair bit past Eight Mile Road—a network of ancient tendrils, tended and strengthened by Charles, all meeting beneath the Detroit River.

I knew that was where Charles would be, drawing upon the sacrifice that was Devil's Night. So I prepared for battle, collecting every weapon at my disposal—a silver dagger that had belonged to my father, Voodoo poisons and tinctures he had taught me to make, and a .44 Magnum as a last resort.

I opened my heart to the pulsing hate beneath the asphalt and concrete, to the hurt pumping through sewers and storm drains where thorny vines absorbed blood and suffering and released rage and madness. I followed that negativity past burning homes and burning churches. I followed it past teenagers fighting like rabid dogs and past good folk crying in the streets.

Last night was the worst it's ever been—Devil's Night, I mean. I knew Charles would be strong when I found him. Too strong maybe, all that bad blood fueling him, so I called upon the storm and solicited the rain. That's when our battle began—before I even reached the river. The rain I'd summoned fought to extinguish the fires he'd instigated. The cold winds and the colder precipitation drove people out of the streets and away from the madness—keeping them from serving as sacrifice to my husband.

Charles fought back, even from afar. He sent his dogs for me—corrupt cops and pre-pubescent gangbangers, but I was invisible in the chaos and the storm. The city loves me as I love it, and my footsteps vanished behind me, even where the ground was caked with wet ash. My pursuers were left scratching their heads.

That trail of darkness ended at an old pump house on the river's edge. Dark vines crawled up the exterior walls, looking as if they might be the only thing holding together the crumbling brick façade. The broken concrete ground had been reclaimed by the earth. It was covered in rich mud and spotted with thorny briar patches.

The barbed vegetation reached out for me as I approached the entrance to the pump house. I could feel the anger and the hunger in those vines, desperate to flay my skin and feast upon my blood, but I willed them away and a clear path presented itself.

No door in this city is locked to me, and it was the same for the pump house. The lock clicked open as soon as my fingers touched the handle. The heady smell of compost and mingling pheromones hit me as I opened the door.

A strange radiance, both beautiful and unsettling, clung about the interior of the building. Violet halos of light, dim and pulsing, hung about the flowering vines that covered the wall and the ceiling. Massive plant pods, like burgundy-colored artichokes the size of basketballs, dotted the brick floor between a maze of massive, rusted pipes.

Large bees with iridescent stripes, some variety I had never seen, buzzed around the pump house, collecting toxic nectar from one flower after the other. The insects made me think twice about going any further. There was something dangerous about them. I could feel the collective aggression of their hivemind and it scared me. The nectar of these flowers had corrupted them.

Scrawled all across the walls in indelible marker, beneath the sprawling flora, were insane ramblings and nonsense equations. I never bothered to study the Black Power occultism that Charles had delved into, but I had enough passing knowledge of it to recognize the "Supreme Mathematics" and the "Supreme Alphabet" represented in the mad writing on the walls.

Charles was nowhere to be seen, but I could feel him deeper within the pump house. I walked through that massive room, toward a pool of brackish water at the far end. The vines edged toward me, eager to strike out, but afraid of my power and pushed back by my will. The neon bees buzzed around my head and I did my best to stay calm and invisible to them, concerned the whole time that my body was leaking out pheromones that would betray my fear.

When I passed the first of the plant pods littering the floor I was shaken with terror and disgust. This close I could see a shape behind the translucent flesh of the pod—the shape of a baby.

I lost my composure at that point, which is a rarity for me. I clawed at the pod with my nails, ripping away wet, fibrous chunks until the thing burst open with a torrent of water. I reached in and took hold of the baby, which was tethered to the plant by a twisted vine that served as an umbilical cord. The child was not being devoured by the plant as I thought but rather incubated by it.

"Beautiful, isn't she?"

I turned to see my husband rising from the dark pool at the far end of the pump house. He was naked, save for the gleam of water on his skin. Dark purple vines lifted him into the air, their venomous thorns biting into his flesh.

"I wish we could have had our own children, back in simpler times. The old-fashioned way, of course, rather than like this."

The vines placed Charles down on the brick floor and retreated into the pool. He walked toward me, his lips upturned into a wide grin. His eyes, once brown and intense, were pools of emerald light.

"What the hell did you do, Charles?"

I clutched the baby to my chest as he approached, unsure if I should protect it from him or smash the unnatural creature against the floor.

"Soon this city will burn to the ground, my love. I will cut away the rot and purge all the poison. And when all this is ash, there will rise a new race of man … a new race of gods … literally born from this sacred soil to build the new Mecca."

I looked back down at the baby that I had freed from the plant. Its features were a mockery of humanity—bulbous eyes beneath lids like hungry mouths and waxy ebony flesh like the skin of an eggplant. It opened its mouth to reveal prickly gums and let out a cry like a dying cat.

Distracted by the child, I had dropped my guard. The vines struck out and lacerated my calf. The venom secreted from the thorns burned like acid.

It took only seconds for the toxin to work its magic. All the resentment for Charles that had built up in my heart bubbled to the surface. My own disappointments and pain clawed to the forefront of my mind. The shade that possessed my husband—the shade that possessed my city—was plunging its hooks into me, trying to dig into my soul.

I threw the baby to the floor in disgust, but a tangle of vines caught the thing and cradled it. For a moment I thought they sought to protect it, but then they constricted around the child and stripped it apart with their thorns. The vines suckled upon the wet ooze inside the thing, taking its essence into themselves.

"She wasn't ripe yet. She never would have made it," Charles said, gesturing toward the rest of the pods. "But there are plenty of others."

His voice made me angry. It reminded me of all the terrible things he had done. It made me think of how he had left me all alone.

I shook my head, trying to banish the crimson haze of rage that was taking over over my mind.

"Charles, baby, this isn't you." I took a deep breath, struggling to remain calm. "There's a shade inside your heart."

"The true spirit of the city is in my heart, and now it is in yours as well."

The Exorcism of Detroit, Michigan

I grew angrier with each word he spoke. What the hell did he know about the true spirit of Detroit? What the hell did he know about me? He'd turned his back on both of us.

With my mind caught in that angry fog, the vines reached out, more and more of them, grappling my limbs and cutting into me. With the last remnants of will at my disposal, I called out for help—a plea to the small creatures of the city save me.

Moments later the pump house was swarming with river rats and feral strays. Flocks of pigeons flew through the broken skylight above. The animals tore at those cursed vines and attacked the violet pods. Charles screamed in rage, commanding the plants and bees to fight back. The pump house became a battlefield from some nightmare version of Doctor Doolittle.

I took the opportunity of the chaos to fight against the rage in my mind. I pushed aside my anger and resentment and focused on the things I love. The sound of Diana Ross singing across the radio waves. The way the moon looks over Book Tower on a clear summer night. My dear husband, lost forever to the demon in his heart.

My own anger, righteous and pure, burned away the venom in my blood along with its artificial rage. I marched through the thorny brambles, ignoring the stings of the neon bees, and approached the thing that wore my husband's skin.

"You can't have him anymore," I said. "You can't have his body. You can't have his power."

The thing that was once my husband howled and a tremor shook the entire pump house. The burgundy vines that ran across the entirety of the building trembled and vibrated like guitar strings. Beehives, hidden in the shadows of the ceiling fell to the ground, releasing their angry swarms.

Vines lashed around my torso, constricting and dragging me toward my husband. The thorns pumped more of that black venom into my blood, trying to overtake my mind.

"We were supposed to save this city together!" Charles growled, pulling me close enough that I could feel his breath.

"We will," I told him as I slipped my daddy's silver knife out from my belt and buried it between his ribs.

The emerald glow in his eyes faded. The tremors shaking the building ceased and the vines constricting over my body went limp. Charles collapsed in my arms, coughing up blood. He looked up at me with those deep brown eyes—the eyes I had fallen in love with so many years ago.

"We were supposed to save this city together," he repeated.

"We will, baby. All you have to do is close your eyes, and I'll do the rest."

I'd like to tell you that Charles faded peacefully in my arms at that point. That isn't how it happened, though. He went into convulsions and blood foamed up from his mouth and nose. His last moments were a flurry of ugly suffering.

The ceasing of the tremors was short-lived. The entire building began to shake in rhythm with my husband's death throes, and the pool at the far end of the pump house erupted into a geyser. What came up from that water I can't rightfully describe, and I am quite sure what I saw of it was just the tip of the iceberg, so to speak.

Its body was like a knot of red seaweed, infused with bones and trash. Torrents of water poured from a dozen snapping jaws like those of a Venus flytrap. Parasites and aquatic insects crawled in and out of its folds and crevices while vines like tendrils thrashed wildly in the air.

It doesn't really matter what the monster looked like; it only matters what it was. And what was it, you ask? It was a shade born of a million forgotten tragedies. It was the evil thing that has poisoned this land since the days before the Injuns. It was the thing that had possessed my city and my man.

The monster flailed its vines around in mindless fury. I retrieved my gun and fired .44 caliber slug into the evil thing, then another and another. I marched forward, accepting the stray blows from the vines and fired two more shots. My gun left some impressive holes, but they were healing shut almost as quickly as I fired.

The Exorcism of Detroit, Michigan

I retrieved one of the poisons my father had taught me to make, a particularly lethal mixture known by few men. I fired a final shot and shoved my hand into the thing's gaping wound, which was already healing. Even as the monster knit its waxy flesh back together around my wrist, I poured the poison into its wound.

Those corrupted bees were swarming me, stabbing their venomous, serrated stingers into my flesh and thrashing vines battered me with thorns, even as I delivered the toxin. My body finally gave in to the lacerations, the venom, and the stings. The world spun in circles around me and I was suddenly lying on my side. I watched as the plant-thing collapsed back into the pool of dark water, its tendrils shriveling.

I could feel its terror.

I could feel it dying.

That made it okay that I too was dying. I'd destroyed the shade who had stolen my husband and I saved Detroit from the parasite that had been eating away at it since time immemorial. Not a bad way to go out.

But I didn't die, of course. The city loves me, you see, just as I love it, and the city saved me. I'm not sure how I got out of the pump house before it collapsed into the river, but I have no doubt it was the spirit of Detroit who left me safe upon the shore where you found me. And I'm confident it was the city itself that purged my body of the venom within it as thanks for my purging of the parasite around its heart.

So there's your confession. This wasn't a murder. This wasn't some Satanic Voodoo terrorist trying to poison the well. This was a goddamn exorcism.

Now you probably won't believe a thing I've written down, but mark my words, life's gonna change around here. With Charles gone, and that thing beneath the city dead, there'll be fewer fires next year, and even less the year after. Soon enough Devil's Night will be nothing but a bad memory—some dark bit of trivia that only comes up in rock songs and horror novels.

But will the city heal? Maybe it will, or maybe there's too much damage done already. Either way, this is still my city and I'm sure as hell gonna do everything I can to make things better. I can't do that from behind bars, though, and like I said earlier no door in this city is locked to me, so I'm afraid I'll be gone by the time you read this. And don't expect me to turn up again. This city will hide me and cover my tracks. But I leave you with this confession and this gift of truth, from one servant of Motor City to another.

Yours truly,
The Dryad of Detroit

About the Author

CURTIS M. LAWSON is a writer of unapologetically weird, dark fiction and poetry. His work includes *Black Heart Boys' Choir, It's a Bad, Bad, Bad, Bad World,* and *The Devoured.*

Curtis is a member of the Horror Writer's Association, and the host of the *Wyrd Transmissions* podcast. He lives in Salem, MA, with his wife and son.

About the Artist

Luke Spooner / Carrion House is an illustrator and artist living in the south of England. **https://carrionhouse.com/**

Made in the USA
Monee, IL
13 September 2021